# *Do Not Resuscitate*

by

Charley Brindley

charleybrindley@yahoo.com

https://www.charleybrindley.com/


Edited by

Karen Boston
https://bit.ly/2rJDq3f


Cover by

Charley Brindley

Printed in the United States of America

First Edition November 2019

This book is dedicated to
**Vern F. Brindley Jr.**


Some of Charley Brindley's books
have been translated into:
Italian
Spanish
Portuguese
French
and
Russian

Other books by Charley Brindley

1.  *Oxana's Pit*
2.  *Raji Book One: Octavia Pompeii*
3.  *Raji Book Two: The Academy*
4.  *Raji Book Three: Dire Kawa*
5.  *Raji Book Four: The House of the West Wind*
6.  *Hannibal's Elephant Girl Book One: Tin Tin Ban Sunia*
7.  *Hannibal's Elephant Girl Book Two: Voyage to Iberia*
8.  *Cian*
9.  *Ariion XXIII*
10.  *The Last Seat on the Hindenburg*
11.  *Dragonfly vs Monarch: Book One*
12.  *Dragonfly vs Monarch: Book Two*
13.  *The Sea of Tranquility 2.0 Book One: Exploration*
14.  *The Sea of Tranquility 2.0 Book Two: Invasion*
15.  *The Sea of Tranquility 2.0 Book Three: The Sand Vipers*
16.  *The Sea of Tranquility 2.0 Book Four: The Republic*
17.  *Sea of Sorrows*
18.  *The Last Mission of the Seventh Cavalry*
19.  *Henry IX*
20.  *Qubit's Incubator*
21.  *Casper's Game*
22.  *The Rod of God*
    Coming Soon
23.  *Dragonfly vs Monarch: Book Three*
24.  *The Journey to Valdacia*
25.  *Still Waters Run Deep*
26.  *Ms Machiavelli*
27.  *Ariion XXIX*
28.  *The Last Mission of the Seventh Cavalry Book 2*
29.  *Hannibal's Elephant Girl, Book Three*

See the end of the book for details about the other books

# Contents


Chapter One ........................................................... 2

Chapter Two............................................................ 6

Chapter Three......................................................... 18

Chapter Four ......................................................... 20

Chapter Five.......................................................... 41

Chapter Six........................................................... 50

Chapter Seven ........................................................ 57

Chapter Eight ........................................................ 60

Chapter Nine ......................................................... 140

# Chapter One

March 23, 2019

I brushed my hand down my face, trying to wipe away the fog that shrouded my mind. As I did, my fingers caught on something stuck in my nose.

*What the hell? Where am I?*

The tube felt like it was halfway down my throat. I tried to pull it out, but it was taped to my face. My brain was stiff, drifting away. I tried to concentrate.

*Still nothing but muddled images. Not a thing I can lock onto. Eyes open, but hazy view of...what? Inside of a cloud. Lots of white stuff and shiny metal. Tubes. Beeping noise.*

*Hospital. Oh, yeah. That doctor who looked like she was about twelve years old. Way too grim for a kid.*

I felt as if I'd been crushed and reconstituted into a piece of crap. Not much pain; just a mind full of wet cement.

*They've got me doped up on painkillers.*

*Just as well.*

*Hope they remember, 'Do Not Resuscitate.' I don't want to hang onto a life of tubes, respirators, and beeping monitors.*

A soft, rustling sound.

*Man in blue, pretty powder blue. Another doctor? Good, not a teenager. Please don't give me any bullshit about a few more years of so-called life. I'm almost eighty. A few more years of misery and hardships for Caitlion isn't what I want. Just snip these tubes and let me go.*

The man in blue pulled a chair to the side of my bed, sat, and smiled.

Not taking vitals, not looking sternly at monitors, no stethoscope draped around his neck, not shoving needles into me; just smiling. Big guy, maybe 6-3, lean, light beard, brown hair, blue eyes, dark blue, like that first shade of night.

"What are you so..." *Ugh, dry throat.* I swallowed. "Chipper about?"

"It's almost time."

His voice was smooth, not as masculine as I expected. It was more like Mom's voice, from when I was a kid. Soft, pleasant, making me feel like everything would be all right.

Another sound. The door swishing open. I turned my head on the pillow to see the nurse.

She checked the monitors. I wondered why the doctor had no interest in the readings.

She tapped a red fingernail on a digital display, then smiled at me, ignoring the doctor.

I tried to return her pleasantness. She was pretty and young, twenty-something. Her complexion was like the soft brown of summer wheat.

"You doing okay, Mr. Brindley?"

I nodded.

"They're going to bring you some nice mush and prune juice. Then the doctor will be in to talk to you."

When I tried to raise my right hand to point to the doctor sitting beside me, it was weighted down by a tube and two needles inserted into the back of my hand.

She was gone before I could say anything.

"You should probably ask to see your family," the doctor said.

"That bad, huh?"

He nodded. "We have to get started."

"If I know my great-granddaughter, she's around here somewhere."

"Sleeping in a chair, out in the waiting room."

"Can you get her?"

"No, you need to push your button."

"Where is it?"

"Right beside your hand."

"Oh, okay."

I fumbled with the button, then pressed it. My nurse hurried in.

"What can I get for you, sweetie?" She put a soft hand on my shoulder. I liked her. She was kind, no nonsense.

"Is Caitlion out there?"

She nodded. "I expect so. She's here more than I am."

*Poor kid. Is she going to be all right? I hope she's prepared. I held on until she turned eighteen. I didn't want other people making her decisions. It'd been just her and me since she was two, when her mom ran away with a trucker from Wichita. In a few weeks, Caitlion will be well-off. Alone, but she can go to university, or to Europe...whatever she wants to do. I know it will be a rough month or so.*

"Papa."

There she was, my beautiful girl, taking my hand and leaning down for a kiss on the cheek. Her name, Caitlion, like Kate Lion, came from her mother's slurred speech when she was high on fentanyl and heroin. She was trying to say, "Tavion," whatever that means.

"Hey, baby."

She wore jeans with manufactured holes and a pink tee saying, '5 out of 4 people struggle with math.'

That made me smile.

"You're looking good today," she said.

Long auburn hair. Her brown eyes were deep, with a hint of mystery about them, as if they hid a special secret. She'd tinted the last six inches of her hair in a light honey blonde, in what I think she called babylights. And always, the beautiful smile.

I blew a puff of air past the tube in my nose and waved my hand, shooing away her words. "I think...this is it, sweetheart."

"No, Papa. It's not." She took my hand, being careful of the IV.

# Chapter Two


August 10, 1945

I slipped in through the door in the back of the classroom and took the only vacant seat.

"Who are you?"

It was my first day at Fordland High School. The squat little man in front of the class stood glaring at me. He was dressed in a dove gray suit, with a black vest and wide floral tie. I'd never seen a male teacher before.

"Ch-Charley Brindley."

"Wonderful. Brindley boy number five. Are there any more of you?"

I didn't know what he meant. Any more brothers, or any more Brindleys? I shook my head.

*Why is everyone looking at me?*

I heard a girl giggle. I slumped down, staring at the huge English textbook on my desk.

*Can I just crawl under it and die?*

"All right." The teacher turned to the blackboard. "We'll try to proceed without the benefit of your input." He picked up a piece of chalk. "Mr. Winter Coldstream," he said as he wrote his name on the board. "Yes, my mother had a great sense of humor."

He dropped the chalk in the tray and dusted his

hands. "Who can name the eight parts of speech?"

Six hands went up. All of them girls.

Mr. Coldstream looked around at the smiling girls. His eyes fell on me. "Brindley?"

No one had ever called me by my last name. I looked down and swallowed.

"Can you name them?"

I didn't even know speech had parts. "Um…" I grabbed my textbook and flipped it open.

"You should have learned this in fourth grade." He looked around the room. "You, what's your name?"

"Ember Coldstream."

"I thought you looked familiar. Name them."

The others lowered their hands.

Ember smiled and named off the parts of speech.

*She's so cute, and smart, too.*

"Very good, Ember." He glanced around the room. "What's an adjective?"

The same six girls raised their hands.

"Brindley?"

*Oh, my God. Why does he keep asking me this stuff?*

I stared at my open book, keeping quiet and not moving, hoping I'd disappear from the surface of the Earth. I felt my face flush, and I knew everyone was watching me, probably laughing to themselves about my stupidity.

"Well, I guess Brindley is so deep into mathematical calculations, his ears have blocked out all external stimuli."

Several kids laughed, one boy louder than the others. I knew who he was.

*Henry Witt. He probably doesn't even know what stimuli is. I sure don't.*

"What's your name?" the teacher asked another student.

"William Dermott."

"All right, William. What's an adjective?"

*Why does he call me by my last name and everyone else by their first?*

"Um..." William looked at his hands, the floor, the window. "Um...a person, place, or thing?"

"Wrong. Does anyone know the part of speech for a person, place, or thing?"

The same six girls again.

Mr. Coldstream strode across the front of the room and stopped before a girl with her hand in the air. "Who are you?"

"Juliet Dermott." She lowered her hand.

"Really? Do you know Mr. William Dermott over there?"

"I wish I didn't." She glared at William.

"Can you answer the question, Juliet?"

"Noun."

*She's pretty, and smart, like Ember.*

"Correct. What are most words ending in '-ly' known as?"

*Please don't ask me again. I don't know any of this stuff.*

"Adverbs," Juliet said.

"Right."

*I never knew time could pass so slowly. Hey, I did an adverb.*

"Let's talk about diagramming a sentence, shall we?" Mr. Coldstream wrote on the board, 'The quick brown fox jumps over the lazy dog.'

*Diagramming? That's about a fox and a dog.*

The fifty-five minutes in Mr. Coldstream's ninth grade English class seemed like fifty-five hours. The ringing of the bell was music to my ears. I grabbed my book and hurried out into the hall.

"Hey, Clod Hopper."

I turned to see a tall boy leaning against the wall. He had red hair and about a thousand freckles.

"What are you doing here?"

Another boy and two girls were with him. They stared at me, waiting for me to say something.

"Going to history class."

"No, what are you doing in high school?"

I didn't know what he meant. I shrugged.

"You're supposed to go to junior high first."

The one-room school I came from had grades one through eight, but no junior high. "Oh."

"What an idiot," the other boy said. It was Henry Witt.

"He doesn't even know what junior high is," Ember said.

All of them laughed at me.

"Love your overalls," Ember said, then giggled.

I turned, wanting to run from the building and go home, but I forced myself to walk away slowly.

*I've got to find my history class.*

I walked down the hall, then turned back.

*I must have missed it.*

I heard some girls singing. "Pee wadley Pasty, huge big fatsy."

Turning a corner in the hallway, I saw a group of four girls facing an overweight girl.

"Pee wadley Pasty, huge big fatsy," they sang, then laughed at the big girl as tears streamed down her cheeks.

The poor girl was backed up against her locker, with no place to go. Her sky-blue eyes were clouded with tears. She wiped her face on her sleeve and turned to lean her head against the locker. Her long blonde hair curled down over her shoulders. She was big, probably over 250 pounds, but why did they tease her?

Other students walked by, some laughing or making mean remarks as they went on their way. I felt as if I should say or do something, but one of those girls was Ember Coldstream. I didn't want her to remind everyone of my humiliation in English class.

Apparently tiring of their torturing of Patsy, the four girls went on their way, still singing their silly ditty. After they left, Patsy opened her locker and found a handkerchief.

*What can I say to the girl? I feel sorry for her, but I'm such a klutz. I'd probably just say something stupid.*

Patsy watched the four girls go into a classroom, then she took some books from her locker. I hesitated, but when she turned and saw me standing there, I hurried away, looking for the history classroom.

* * * * *

The lunch hour was an even worse experience.

"What's that smell?" said a boy at the next table.

"Cow shit," said another.

"Where's it coming from?"

"Oh, look, it's the plow boy."

"What are you doing in here, Clod Hopper?"

I looked down at the egg sandwich Mom had made for me.

"I think he's eating a cow shit sandwich."

The other boys laughed, drawing attention from the next table.

"I thought brown-baggers were supposed to eat outside?"

"Yep, that's the rule."

"Probably when he learns the parts of speech," a girl said, "he'll be able to read the rulebook."

I knew who it was without looking—Ember.

"Didn't they make a rule book with pictures," she said, "so the farmers can figure out the regulations?"

That got her a round of laughter.

"Yeah," a boy said, "a coloring book."

I rolled the rest of my sandwich in the paper bag and grabbed my thermos of milk.

"Oh, no. He's about to cry."

They boo-hooed and tossed off more smart remarks as I hurried from the cafeteria.

I couldn't get away fast enough, and I sure wasn't hungry anymore.

*That's the last time I'll go there for lunch. Is there really a rule about not taking your lunch into the cafeteria? Maybe if I eat there, I have to buy my lunch. If I had lunch money, I would. Tomorrow, I'll go outside at lunchtime to see if anyone else brings their lunch from home.*

* * * * *

"Mom, I don't want to go to school."

It was the morning after my first day of high school.

"Why?" She worked on my sandwich for lunch.

"Everyone hates me."

"I don't think they hate you."

"They picked on me all day, even at lunch."

"Did you tell them to leave you alone?"

I shook my head and took a bite of Post Toasties and milk, then added another teaspoon of sugar.

"When they say something mean to you, say something back."

"But I can never think of anything until it's all over. After they laugh and walk away, then I think of a comeback."

"Well, you have to think faster."

*Yeah, good idea, Mom. But my brain is too slow for that.*

"How about if I just punch them in the face? Except for the girls."

"The girls are mean, too?"

"Yes."

*There's no way I'm gonna talk to a girl. Or punch one, although I'd rather do that than talk to them.*

"Where are you when they pick on you?"

"In the hallway, and at lunchtime in the cafeteria."

"Okay, when a class ends, stay in the classroom until just a minute before the next class, then hurry to the next one before they have time to say anything. And find a quiet place to eat lunch. You don't have to go to the cafeteria for lunch."

"Good idea, Mom."

I took my lunch sack and ran to catch the school bus.

* * * * *

At lunchtime, I grabbed my sandwich from the locker and hurried outside, where I wandered around until I came to the football field. I climbed the steps and sat in the middle of the empty bleachers.

As I unwrapped my egg sandwich from the wax paper, I noticed someone across the field, in the middle of the other set of bleachers. From her size, I knew it was Patsy. I thought about going over to ask if I could eat with her, but someone sat beside her. It was a girl with metal braces on both legs.

I could see they were talking while they ate, so I decided not to intrude. Besides, I didn't know how to intrude.

*Do I just walk over and sit down? Or ask if I could sit with them? What if they say, 'No?' Then what? That would be embarrassing. Better to keep to myself.*

After a quick lunch, I went to my science classroom a half-hour early and sat in the empty room, where it was quiet. Twenty-five minutes later, when the kids started coming in, I pretended to read my textbook.

"Wow," one of the boys said, "he knows how to read."

"Na, he's got a comic book hidden inside his science book."

They laughed.

*I should say something. What's a good comeback? "Yeah, I got Superman in here." No, that's stupid. "Sure, don't you wish you had one in yours?" No, that requires an answer, and he'd have a smart remark, then I'd have to think of another one. My God, social life's complicated. I'll just keep quiet until they get tired of pestering me. How long's that going to take? Probably the whole semester. Crap, three months of teasing, pestering, and wisecracks. I'll never make it. How does Patsy do it?*

Mrs. Adams's history class had some of the same students from my English class.

I sat in the back, hoping no one would notice.

After the teacher wrote 330 BC on the blackboard, she asked, "Where did Alexander the Great come from?"

Several students raised their hands.

She went to stand in front of a girl. "What's your name?"

"Ember Coldstream."

"Can you answer the question?"

"I think Brindley knows. He's an expert on ancient history." She turned to grin at me.

*What? Why is she doing this to me?*

"Brindley," Mrs. Adams said, "where did Alexander the Great come from?"

"Um...England?"

"No. Anyone?"

Juliet raised her hand. Mrs. Adams nodded to her.

"Macedonia."

"Right. And what empire was the first to be conquered by him?"

"Greece."

"Right again. Good work. I'm glad someone's been reading during summer vacation. Now, let's talk about the Roman Empire."

Before the class was over, she assigned us the first three chapters to read before the next day's class.

* * * * *

Algebra was just as hard as English and history.

*Why didn't Mrs. Caldwell teach us some of this stuff?*

"*Buenas tardes estudiantes*," (Good afternoon, students) Mrs. Sandoval said at the beginning of Spanish class.

Several kids responded, "*Buenas tardes, Señora Sandoval.*"

"*Es un hermoso día*," (It's a beautiful day) Ember said.

I sat in the back of the room, staying very still. I had no idea what Ember had said, but it brought a smile to the teacher's face.She then looked my way, and I sank down, knowing what was coming.

"*Como te llamas, joven?*" (What's your name, young man?)

I only knew by her tone of voice that she'd asked a question. I shook my head.

"I asked your name."

"Oh, Charley Brindley."

"*El tiene un ligero problema mental,*" (He has a slight mental problem) Ember said.

A few of the students giggled.

I only knew it was something about a mental problem; I could guess the rest.

"*Oh, siento mucho escuchar eso,*" (Oh, I'm so sorry to hear that) Mrs. Sandoval said. "We'll start off slow for your benefit."

Ember's smile looked very much like a sneer.

*Why does she hate me?*

I opened my textbook and held it up in front of my face.

* * * * *

After school, I stood on the sidewalk, waiting for the school bus.

"Back of the line, Clod Hopper."

"What?" It was the freckle-faced Crammer.

"You're standing in my spot. Get to the back of the line, where you belong."

"There's no line."

"There will be, and you're in my spot."

He shoved me backwards, knocking my books to the ground.

Some other kids came to watch.

I lunged for him, grabbing him around the waist.

15

Crammer brought up his knee, hitting me in the stomach.

When I swung at him, he hit me in the chest, knocking me down.

The others laughed. "Go get him, Brindley."

I jumped up and swung my right fist.

He turned his shoulder toward me.

My fist hit solid muscle.

He punched me in the face, and I went down. I got to my knees, rubbing my eye.

The bus pulled up, and everyone filed on, laughing at me as they passed me. I was last to board. I dropped into a seat behind the driver.

* * * * *

After a month in school, I'd learned nothing, except for the best places to hide at lunchtime and to keep quiet in class. The teachers finally quit asking me questions, since I could never answer anything correctly.

It was the same in all six subjects. I sat in the back and just tried not to be noticed. I took notes and read my assignments, but I was just too slow. Most of the other kids participated in class, always ready to show off their knowledge, particularly the girls – and especially Ember. I guess because her father was a teacher.

* * * * *

I left English, hurrying toward my history class.

"Hay Seed."

I turned to see Crammer coming toward me, followed closely by his gang of three.

*Oh, no. Not again.*

"What?"

"You wear those same overalls every day?"

I looked down at myself. Actually, I had four pair. Mom washed clothes three times a week. We had a wringer washing machine on the back porch. Dad and my uncle Leo had rigged up an old electric motor they'd salvaged from a junk yard, to rotate the drum paddle. But all my overalls did look alike.

"And the same flour sack shirt?" he asked.

"Yeah, I-I guess so."

"Tell your old lady to use a burlap bag next time. That's more your style."

He turned to grin at his pals. They laughed. He looked back at me, waiting, I guess, for a response.

I didn't have one.

# Chapter Three

March 23, 2019

"Caitlion, just listen to me. We've had a good eighteen years. Now, you're going out there and live your life. Go to university, run the company, travel…but promise me you won't squander your life. Live it to the fullest, for me."

"Charley," the man said. "It's time."

I nodded.

My little Caitlion held my wrinkled old hand to her cheek. "I can't let you go."

"You have to, baby. He said it's time."

I waved a hand toward him. She looked around, as if no one else was there.

"I want you to…" I stopped for a breath. "…go get me a Big Mac. Can you do that?"

She sniffed and smiled. "Will they let you have it?"

"The nurse said I could have anything I want today." That wasn't true, but it really didn't matter.

She stood. "I'll be back in ten minutes. You want fries?"

I nodded and gave her my last smile, then she left the room.

"When you arrive, look for this iPad in the loft of the barn," the blue doctor said. "It's loaded with everything; Encyclopedia Britannica, Wikipedia…" He glanced at the glowing screen before him, which illuminated his face in a greenish light. He slid his finger up to the next page. "Every book in the Library of Congress, every invention in the U.S. Patent Office, formulas and descriptions of every medicine known to man, and a lot more you'll find when you need it. There'll be a solar charging panel, too. You have to keep everything hidden. They would never understand."

"What loft? What barn?" I asked.

"The round barn. You know how to work the notebook, right?"

"Yeah, but I can't even walk. Are they going to take me in an ambulance?"

"No, you're going to fly."

I almost laughed. "Oh, okay."

"We only have a few minutes. All your instructions will be in a folder named 'Instructions.'"

*How clever to disguise the name like that. I never would have figured that out.*

"Instructions for what?"

"You'll see when you get there."

"What kind of doctor...are you?" My heart did some kind of flip-flop I'd never felt before. Not painful, but disconcerting. My breath stopped for a few seconds.

"...before she gets back," he said.

"Wha—" Tingling, my legs.

"...but you won't be able to contact us."

"Contact who?"

What a strange feeling. Something warm flowing through me.

I heard some erratic beeps, then a long one.

I felt a *whoosh*, like air pushed out of a tunnel ahead of a speeding train.

Then a jolt.

# Chapter Four

September 27, 1945

I felt a jolt, like an electric shock. But there was no pain; just a quick buzz inside my head, then tingling throughout my body. It felt as if all the blood had been sucked out of me and instantly replaced with new blood interlaced with some sort of effervescent bubbly substance. It actually felt pretty good, and my vision sharpened to crystal clarity. I closed my eyes for a moment, savoring the new feeling, then opened my eyes to see the ugly face of Justin Crammer.

"You hear me, asshole?"

"What did you say about my mom?"

"I said, your old lady can't sew for shit."

He glanced at Ember and his two boy pals, then grinned. He turned back and grabbed me by the collar.

I didn't even think; just reacted. Gripping his hand, I put pressure on the back kof his wrist and twisted it to the side.

He went to his knees, crying out.

When he balled his other hand into a fist and swung at me, I twisted more, putting him on the floor.

*Damn, where did that come from?*

I let him go and stepped back.

*I could've broken his wrist.*

He struggled to stand but only got one knee under himself. Ember reached to take his arm, but he shook her off.

"Get away from me," he told her, then stood. "I'll get you for this, Brindley."

"Okay. How're you going to do that?"

"You'll find out."

"How about push-ups, right now?"

"What?"

"The one of us who does the most in five minutes, wins."

Someone behind him laughed.

*Yeah, I know, he's the strongest player on the football team.*

Crammer grinned, dropped to the floor, and positioned himself on his hands.

I handed my books to Ember and fell beside him.

We began together.

At ten, I started counting aloud.

When we hit fifteen, he slowed a little.

The other kids cheered him on.

At thirty, I said, "One-hand."

"What?"

I put my left hand behind my back and kept going.

Crammer did the same.

He got to thirty-five, then fell on his chest, breathing hard.

I continued, pushing easily with my right arm.

"Forty," I said, then stood and held out my hand.

He knocked it away. "This ain't over."

"Oh, now what?"

"You just better watch out."

I glanced at Ember and lifted a shoulder. She did the same.

"Watch out." She mouthed the words, then handed over my books, with a smile.

The bell rang.

Crammer stomped away, followed by Ember and his pals.

* * * * *

In history class, I took my usual seat in the back. Strange visions filled my mind, like dreaming while awake.

*A war in the jungle...a wide river flowing through the rainforest...an oasis in the desert...skiing...*

It was like a long movie set to super fast motion.

*A smoky bar room...guitar music...me singing...*

"Brindley?"

I looked up to see Mrs. Adams standing at the front of the classroom and all the students watching me, some smiling, probably expecting me to sink down in my chair and not say a word, like I always did.

"Yes, ma'am?" I said.

"I asked, who crossed the Alps to attack the Romans in two-sixteen BC?"

*That's a dumb question. Is she serious?*

I just stared at her.

"That's what I thought," Mrs. Adams said. "Anyone?"

Several hands went up.

"Hannibal," I said, then folded my arms.

"What?" the teacher asked.

"He took thirty-nine elephants and twenty-six thousand soldiers," I said. "The army was divided into ten thousand cavalry and sixteen thousand foot soldiers. Probably a few hundred camp followers as well."

"Huh?"

"Most of the elephants died in the cold in the higher elevations." I glanced around at the other students.

22

Ember's mouth fell open, and the ones with their hands up, dropped them. "He also lost almost ten thousand troops." I picked up my yellow pencil and twirled it in my fingers.

Mrs. Adams cleared her throat. "That's the most you've said all semester."

"Probably." I opened my textbook and flipped pages, using the eraser on my pencil.

*What was the name of that lake where Hannibal fought his third battle in Italy? I should know this.*

I came across a picture of the Alps.

*Zugspitze! The highest mountain in Bavaria.*

I glanced out the window and watched an elm tree shudder in the wind.

*There's a gold-plated cross on the peak. Kabilis and I climbed up there. When? Who's Kabilis?*

"That's not in the textbook." Mrs. Adams came toward me, with the history textbook held against her ample breasts.

"What?"

"About the elephants dying in the cold."

"But they did."

"I know, but it's not in the book."

"Oh."

"How did you know that?"

"I-I think I read it in the library."

"Since when do you go to the library?"

"Um...during my lunch hour. Maybe it was in Levy or Herodotus."

"Hmm...so you've read Herodotus's Histories?"

I nodded.

"Where was Hannibal's first battle after he crossed the Alps?"

"On the River Trebbia."

"The second one?"

"Ticino."

She opened her history book to where a slip of paper marked a page, then scanned down the sentences. "What was the biggest battle he fought in Italy?"

"Cannae. Fifty thousand Romans died in a single day."

"Yes." She looked from her book to me. "Yes, that's true." She turned to go back to the front of the class, but everyone still stared at me.

*Bavaria. When was I in Bavaria? With Kabilis. We learned to ski that winter. He was a Tech Sergeant, U.S. Air Force. What the hell? He was fluent in German and Russian. I was a Master Sergeant. When...*

The bell rang for lunchtime.

The others shuffled out. I didn't move; couldn't move. My head hurt from the intense pressure. So full of stuff. Jumbled. Swirling like the inside of a tornado.

"Charley."

I jerked up my head. Mrs. Adams stood, watching me.

"Yes, ma'am?"

"Class is over."

"Oh, okay."

I collected my books and stood, walking in a dream. My mind was mesmerized, dazed.

*What's going on?*

In the hallway, I ignored the kids, but I knew they were watching me. I went mechanically to my locker, took my lunch, and went outside, then headed to the bleachers.

There, I saw Patsy and the disabled girl. I went to their side of the stadium.

"Do you mind if I sit with you?" I asked.

They looked up at me, wide-eyed.

"Um...sure," Patsy said.

I sat and took out my sandwich.

The two girls continued to stare, not eating or speaking.

"What kind of sandwich do you have?" I asked.

The girls looked at each other.

"Peanut butter and jelly," Patsy said.

"Me, too," the other one said.

"I've got fried egg. My mom always cuts my sandwich into two triangles. Isosceles, I think." This was the most I'd ever said to a girl, or any kid at school.

Both girls giggled.

"Mine, too," the other girl said.

"You want to share?" I held out half my sandwich.

"Sure."

We traded. "What's your name?" I asked.

"Melody."

"Melody, like a song."

"Yeah. My mom was a singer."

"Really?"

She nodded and bit into the egg sandwich. "This is good." She lifted the bread. "Your mom put mayonnaise, salt, and pepper on it."

"You're 'Charley Brindley,'" Patsy said.

"Yes. Mom calls me 'Charley Eye.' You're 'Patsy McCarthy.'"

"I guess everyone knows me because I'm so fat."

"I knew you because you're in my science class. Do you read a lot?"

"I love to read."

"Me, too," I said. "This grape jelly is really sweet. I like it."

My brain seemed to warm as it hummed. It was very pleasant, watching it fill with memories. But it was also disturbing.

*Where is all this coming from? Has it been there all along and I just couldn't find it?*

"Is your mind full of memories?" I asked Melody.

"Sure," she said. "I can remember everything back to when I was about two. Nothing before that."

"I'm the same," Patsy said. "I wonder why we can't remember things from when we were babies?"

My memories seemed to be of the future, rather than the past.

*Things yet to happen? How can that be?*

"Do you have memories, like, from your future self?" I asked.

"I daydream a lot," Patsy said. "About things I want to do after high school."

"We better go," Melody said. "It's almost class time."

We walked together toward the building, going slow because of Melody's braces.

Inside the school, we were met with a chorus of 'Pee Waldy Patsy.'

"Hey," I whispered to the two girls, "let's throw it back at them."

I told them what we should do. They smiled and nodded.

"Ember and Justin, sitting in a tree," we chanted, "K-I-S-S-I-N-G. First comes love, then comes marriage, then comes Ember with a baby carriage."

It was a silly childhood ditty, but it had the desired effect. Several kids laughed.

Ember was stunned for a moment. "Pee Waldy…"

We sang the kissing song again and advanced on the four girls.

Ember stopped, swallowed her next words, then turned to hurry away. Her three friends followed.

"Good job," I said to Patsy and Melody.

"That felt good," Patsy said.

"Yes, it did," I said. "Lunch tomorrow?"

"Heck, yeah," they said together.

* * * * *

P.E. was the last class of the day. I hated it. I was almost six feet tall, strong, my muscles well-toned from working on the farm. But I didn't know what to do with my strength.

Sometimes we ran the track or did side-straddle-hops; anything for exercise.

This time, we went to the gym to practice basketball.

I sat on the bleachers, still trying to sort my stampeding thoughts. I was in a war, in a jungle, but it wasn't World War II, the one that had just ended. This was unlike anything I'd seen in the newsreels. The uniforms were different; some were just flak jackets over green tees and fatigue trousers. And the weapons. They, or we, didn't carry heavy M-1 rifles...they were smaller, lightweight.

*M-16s!*

*An aircraft flew over us, low, just above the jungle canopy. Very fast. It dropped napalm on an enemy position ahead of us.*

*That's an Navy F-4 jet fighter plane. What the heck is happening to me?*

"Brindley!" Coach Jameson shouted. "Care to join us?"

"Yes, sir." I jumped up and ran onto the court.

The coach was a great guy. He always treated me like a regular kid, even though I was awkward and clumsy.

Coach tossed the basketball to me. I caught it and turned it in my hands.

*I've done this before. Where? When? Vietnam...Da Nang. What the heck?*

I spun the ball, then dribbled it.

Crammer came to stand in front of me. He took a defensive stance.

I watched his eyes as I bounced the ball.

He grinned, then went for the ball.

I stepped to the side. He followed my movement. I faked to the right, then went left, still dribbling. He was off-balance. I took a jump shot. The ball swished through the hoop.

Everyone stopped to stare at me.

I ran to get the ball, then dribbled it away from the hoop, turned, and made another jump shot. Perfect.

Crammer ran for the ball, dribbled it out to mid-court.

I ran for him.

He grinned and started toward the hoop.

I swatted the ball away from him, dribbled around two other players, and made a layup.

When the ball came down from the hoop, I grabbed it and passed it to another player.

*Playing on a dirt court at the military camp in Vietnam. Very hot. Kabilis and I had cut our camo trousers into shorts. Six GIs on the court. Three of us had pulled off our regulation issue green tees and tossed them aside. Shirts and skins, we called the two teams.*

The boy I'd passed the ball to, dribbled, took a jump shot, and missed.

I got the rebound, then threw the ball one-handed, bouncing it off the backboard. It ringed the hoop, then fell through.

*The Marine commander gave us two weeks' furlough. Kabilis and I went to Bangkok. We met...*

Crammer bent his knees, raised the ball for a jump shot. Just as he released the ball, I jumped to take it out of the air, then dribbled out and made the shot he tried to make.

We played hard for thirty minutes.

The other players slowly dropped out, sitting on the floor, catching their breath.

Crammer continued to dog me, trying to get the ball.

I ran for the hoop, bouncing the ball. He tripped me from behind. I went down hard but held onto the ball.

*Gunfire, mortar exploding all around us.*

I stood, still holding the ball under my arm.

*We were cut off in the jungle. I was a medic, working on a wounded soldier. More gunfire from the edge of the clearing, Kabilis went down, bleeding bad.*

"Brindley!" Crammer said. "Come on." He tried to swat the ball from my arm.

I passed it behind myself, to my other hand.

*We fought the Viet Cong all night, losing three of our men, plus six wounded. What happened to Kabilis?*

I tossed the ball to Crammer and went toward the bleachers, where I sat with my head in my hands.

"Charley." The coach sat beside me. "You okay?"

*No, something's wrong with me.*

"Yeah, I'm fine."

"Johnson," the coach said. "Bring that exercise pad. I think Charley better lie down for a few minutes."

*Pad? iPad! That blue doctor, in the hospital, said there was an iPad in the loft of a round barn.*

The bell rang for the end of the class. The school day was over.

"You sure you're all right?"

"I'm good, Coach." I stood. "Don't worry. I was

just...um...thinking about my Spanish assignment."

On the sidewalk, I waited for the bus, trying to sort out my thoughts.

*So many weird things. Some guy in a hospital room, dressed in a light blue suit. He's the one who told me about the iPad in the loft of the round barn. An iPad is a computer. What's a computer?*

Someone came to stand behind me. I glanced around; Crammer.

*I hope he starts something about his place in line. This time, he'll be the one on the ground.*

"Where did you learn to play basketball?"

*In the Marines*, I wanted to say. *Wait a minute; I was a Master Sergeant in the Air Force. How did I get in the Marines, and in Vietnam? Where the heck is Vietnam? Oh, yeah. Southeast Asia.*

"Um, I've got four brothers. We play ball in the backyard."

"You going out for the team?"

"I don't know."

I saw Patsy and Melody come out the double doors of the school building. I waved to them. They waved back, smiling.

Crammer turned that way. "Friends of yours?"His expression looked like he'd just gotten a whiff of something rotten.

"Yeah," I said. "They are." I walked toward the girls. "You can have my place in line," I said over my shoulder.

"Hey," Patsy said.

"Hi. Which bus do you girls ride?"

"Um...three," Melody said. "But we walk home."

"How far is it?" I asked.

"About two miles."

"That's a long walk."

"Better than riding the bus," Patsy said.

I looked toward the place where bus number three would pull up. Ember stood in line, talking to Henry Witt.

"Let me guess," I said, "Ember and her gang like to serenade you on the bus?"

Patsy nodded.

The four school buses pulled up, and the kids began to file on.

"I've got to get home to start on my chores," I said.

"Don't forget lunch," Melody said.

"Right. See you two in the bleachers tomorrow."

* * * * *

I found Mom in the kitchen, working on supper. I kissed her cheek.

"How was school today?"

"Good. Very good."

"Really?"

I nodded. "I'm going to start on chores. I have a lot of homework tonight."

"I thought you hated homework?"

"I have some interesting assignments. History and poetry."

She stared at me for a moment, then smiled. "Can you gather some eggs for me?"

"Sure."

I grabbed the egg basket and headed outside. On the porch steps, I stopped to look across the backyard, past the clothesline and beyond the blacksmith shop. There stood our barn. It was huge because Dad stored a lot of hay for the winter. It was also different than most barns; it was round.

*How'd that blue doctor know about our round*

*barn? And if there really is an iPad in the loft, everything just got a lot weirder.*

In the barn, I climbed the ladder.

*Wow, tons of hay.*

I glanced around the huge loft.

*Surely, they left me a clue; otherwise, I'll never find it.*

Lots of old harnesses hung on the walls. Cobwebs everywhere.

*Spiders have been at work here for decades.*

An old coal oil lantern, broken doubletree, leather mule collar stuffed with straw...all covered in dust and cobwebs.

*Wait a minute.*

I waded through the hay to the lantern. It was perfectly clean; no dust, no spider webs.

*That hasn't been here very long. A lantern lighting the way?*

I cleared the hay, down to the floorboards—and there it was: A cardboard box, just about the right size. And two more boxes.

Inside the first one, I found an iPad.

I sat back against the wall, stunned.

That guy at the hospital, he said I'd find the computer here.

*So, that was a dream?*

I was seventy-nine years old, dying. He knew I'd end up here, my home when I was fourteen. I'm in my body as a teenager, but I have all my memories and knowledge of seventy-nine years!

*This is one hell of a hallucination, and so elaborate.*

I glanced around. Every detail perfectly recreated.

*I died before Caitlion got back with my Big Mac.*

*That must be what happened. Then what is this? Afterlife? No, I don't believe in any of that crap. I'm lying in that hospital bed, hooked up on wires and tubes. Damn it. 'Do Not Resuscitate.' What's the point of signing a legal document if no one reads it? I should have had it tattooed on my forehead.*

My body died, and they're pumping life support shit through my veins. My brain is alive but hopped up on painkillers. And my mind, with no control over my dead body, has to do something.

*So, I'm constructing this elaborate fantasy to entertain myself?*

Two minds. Conscious and subconscious. When we sleep, the subconscious takes over, feeding dreams to the comatose conscious part. Now I'm inside the subconscious, playing this ridiculous game of reliving my high school years.

*How long can it go on?*

Until Caitlion gets back from McDonalds. She'll tell them to pull the plug. She knows very well I don't want to exist as a vegetable.

*How much time do I have?*

In here, in my fantasy, time may not matter. And I won't even know when they cut my life support.

*Until that happens, I'm going to enjoy this little piece of make-believe.*

I opened the iPad and tapped the screen.

*Uh-oh. Password.*

*He didn't tell me the password.*

*Probably in the 'Instructions' folder, which I can't get to without the password.*

Down in the lower right corner of the screen was a stylized thumbprint.

*Could it be?*

I wiped my hand on my overalls and pressed my thumb to the icon.

*Bam!*

'Hello, Charley.'

They—or I—had thought of everything.

I found the 'Instructions' folder and opened the file called 'Instructions.'

*Hard to miss that.*

'One. You are not immune to anything. There are very few vaccines in 1945. Measles, mumps, diphtheria, and especially polio, are all prevalent. You can probably get a small pox shot. Remember, don't touch sick people, and wash your hands often.'

*Polio, I bet that's what Melody has.*

'Two. You can't tell anyone about your mission. They'll think you're crazy, and you'll be locked away in an insane asylum.'

*Mission? What mission?*

'Three. Your mission is to prevent global warming.'

*Oh, is that all?*

'When you left 2019, the world was already past the tipping point. Icecaps were melting, sea levels rising, climate warming at an accelerated rate. Two hundred years from now, the Earth will start correcting that, but the human race will be long gone.'

*That's not good.*

'You have to start the change to green energy—wind and solar.'

*I'm just a kid. What can I do?*

'You're only fourteen years old, but you have all the knowledge of mankind at your fingertips. All you have to do is design a wind turbine and solar panel.'

*Yeah, right. Any teenager could do that.*

'And lastly, don't forget to wash your hands.'

*That's it? All I have to do is stay alive and invent technology from fifty years in the future?*

Polio. Wow, I forgot about that. When I was little, I saw lots of kids in leg braces. I wonder how old Dr. Salk is in 1945. He has to get to work on his polio vaccine.

*I don't want to end up in an iron lung.*

I clicked on the tab for Wikipedia.

*And Albert Einstein. I need to talk to him, too.*

I read about obesity and polio. One link led to another. Cause and effect. History of research. Treatment and cures. Polio is caused by a virus, obesity caused by many things. Polio is highly contagious.

Before I knew it, an hour had passed.

"Charley Eye! Where are you?"

*Oh, no! Mom. The eggs!*

"Coming, Mom."

"What are you doing up there?"

I clicked off the iPad, put it in the box, and covered it with hay.

"Looking for eggs."

"The chickens can't get up there."

I climbed down the ladder. "Sometimes they fly up there."

"Yeah? Let's gather some so I can finish supper. Your dad will be home soon."

* * * * *

During lunch in the bleachers, Patsy, Melody and I talked about the classes we shared. Melody and I had English together. All three of us were in the same history and Spanish classes. Patsy and I had science.

"Can we study history together," I said, "after school?"

35

"Sure." Melody pulled her coat collar tight against the cold wind. "It would be much easier with the three of us working together."

"I know," Patsy said. "I'm always running into words I don't understand."

"Okay," I said. "Where?"

"Me and Patsy live next door to each other, so maybe at one of our houses?"

"That works for me," I said.

"I'll ask Mom if we can study at my house," Patsy said. "But I'm pretty sure it'll be okay."

"Cool." I folded my empty brown bag and shoved it into my hip pocket.

"Cool?" Melody asked.

"Yeah, fine, good, cool."

"Okay, cool."

"We better go," I said. "Lunch hour is almost over."

As we walked toward the school building, I said. "Hey, watch this."

I ran for the flagpole, grabbed it with my left hand, swung around in the air, then gripped higher up with my right hand. I then air-walked up, moving my feet as if they were going up a wall. When I was vertical, I air-walked back down, then back-flipped to the ground.

"Wow!" Patsy said. "How'd you learn that?"

I noticed a few other kids had stopped to watch. "Um...it's just something I learned in our backyard."

"That was really...cool," Melody said.

"So cool, it was almost cold," Patsy said.

We laughed, then hurried for the doors as the bell rang.

* * * * *

The next day at lunch, I sat with Patsy and Melody in the bleachers.

"Mom said we can study at my house," Patsy said. "She wants you and Melody to come to supper tomorrow night, then we can use the dining room to study."

"Awesome," I said. "How about you, Melody?"

"Yeah, I'll be there. Can we work on Spanish, too?"

"Sure. What's your address, Patsy?' I asked. "I'll tell my dad to come pick me up around nine tomorrow night. How's that?"

She gave me her address, and I wrote it on my lunch bag.

"You want to walk home with us tomorrow?" Patsy asked.

I thought about that for a moment as I studied her address. I didn't mind walking, but it seemed a shame since the school bus went right by her house.

"Okay."

* * * * *

The next day after school, the three of us started down the street, walking toward Patsy's house.

"Wait a minute," I said.

Patsy and Melody stopped, turning toward me.

"We're taking bus number three."

"No," Patsy said. "I'd rather walk."

"If you walk home every day, Ember wins. You know that."

"I don't care if she wins. I hate that song."

"We can sing, too," I said.

Melody smiled and nodded.

"I don't—" Patsy began.

"How about if we sing a different song?"

"What song?"

I told them what I was thinking of. We then joined the line waiting for bus number three. Ember was ahead of us, talking and laughing with her friends. She didn't notice us.

The bus pulled up, and the kids filed on. We were the last ones.

"Hey," Ember shouted, "look who's here, the Three Stooges."

That got her a few laughs.

Patsy and Melody sat together. I took the seat in front of them. As soon as the bus pulled away, Ember started in on us.

"Pee wadley Patsy..."

I began singing. Patsy and Melody joined me.

"Not last night, but the night before, twenty-four robbers came knocking at my door..."

Ember raised voice as her friends joined her.

We continued the old jump rope song, only louder. Several other kids sang with us.

Ember stood. "Pee wadley Patsy..."

We stood and started the song from the beginning. Soon, half the kids were standing, singing with us.

Ember sat and folded her arms, staring at me.

Ten minutes later, the bus stopped in front of Patsy's house, and I followed the girls off the bus. When I passed the driver, he was smiling.

* * * * *

"This is really great stew, Mrs. McCarthy."

"Thank you, Charley."

I passed the bread to Patsy, who handed it to

38

Melody without taking any for herself.

During the meal, I asked Mr. McCarthy about his work.

"I work at the office. Just got promoted to assistant postmaster."

"That's pretty good."

"Yeah, took me ten years to make it."

"How much does it cost to mail a letter to Holland?" I asked.

"You can mail it for three cents and it would take a month to get there. Airmail is six cents, but it goes much faster, probably four days."

"That's worth three cents more."

"Do you know someone in Holland?" Patsy asked.

"No, but I would like to write to Mr. Lou Ottens in Bellingwolde, Holland."

"Who is he?" Melody sipped her iced tea.

"He's a famous engineer. I'd like to see if he'll correspond with me."

After supper, I carried the dirty dishes to the kitchen, where Mrs. McCarthy cleaned the stove.

"Patsy didn't eat much tonight," I said.

"She never does. A few bites at breakfast, her sandwich at lunch, and then not much at suppertime."

"Sometimes she doesn't finish her sandwich at lunch," I said.

"She eats like a bird, yet she's so heavy."

"Has she always been that way?"

"Since she was three years old," Mrs. McCarthy said.

"Has anyone ever mentioned hypothyroidism to you?"

She paused, with her hands deep in the dishwater. "What?"

"Hypothyroidism is a medical condition where the thyroid gland–right here, in the neck–doesn't produce enough of the thyroid hormone, which causes weight gain, even though someone eats very little."

"How do you know that?"

"I read it in the school library."

"I've never heard of it."

"She needs to see a doctor," I said. "That may not be the problem, but if it is, it can be treated with a drug called Levothyroxine."

She handed me a plate to dry. "You read about that, too?"

I nodded. "It's been around since 1927. I think they administer it by injection."

# Chapter Five

On my way to social studies, I passed the music room. I turned back and peeked in; no one was in there.

*I wonder.*

I glanced at the kids hurrying by, then pulled open the door and went in.

The instruments leaned in their stands; a bass fiddle, trombone, violin, guitar. A baby grand piano stood in the center of the room.

At the piano, I ran my fingers along the keys, then sat on the bench.

*I know how to play!*

After dropping my books on the floor, I pecked out the first ten bars of *Scarborough Fair*. My fingers remembered. I positioned my hands and began another piece of music, one of my favorites.

As the sweet notes filled the air, a dusty memory slowly came to life. She sat beside me on the piano bench, teaching me to play. Her hands were soft on mine when I made a mistake, gently correcting me. Pretty, heart-shaped face, dark eyes, beautiful smile. It wasn't a baby grand; just an ancient upright piano. Another mistake on the keys. She took my hand, kissed my fingers.

*Now they'll get it right*, she whispered.

My heart fluttered again, just as it did that spring day in Rio De Janeiro.

Music filled the classroom, billowing and ebbing, like clouds of memories and a sea of sorrows and regret. Ebbing and flowing away into the vast emptiness of loss and what might have been.

I played the last note, leaving my finger on the key, letting the sweet sound die away.

*Catalina! Her name was Catalina.*

Applause from behind yanked me from a newborn memory of Catalina standing before me.

*An apartment in Madrid. Midsummer, the heat stifling. Our windows were open, but the air between us stood still, suffocating, like the words she'd just spoken to me. Her backpack sat on the floor at her feet.*

I turned to see several students had crowded through the door. More stood behind them, all clapping their hands.

Mr. Landers, the music teacher, pushed through the kids.

"That's Beethoven," he said as he came toward me.

"Yes, *Fur Elise.* I'm sorry."

"Where did you learn that?"

"I-I don't remember." Ember stood with the others. When I felt my face flush, I grabbed my books from the floor. "I have to go to Spanish class."

"Come see me after classes," Mr. Landers said.

"Yes, sir."

*Am I in trouble?*

The students parted like the Red Sea. I hurried through them and down the hall.

*What happened to Catalina? What happened to*

*me?*

* * * * *

After my last class, I went to see Mr. Landers in the music room. One student was in the room; a girl practicing on her flute.

"What else can you play on the piano?" Mr. Landers asked.

"Um...maybe that one." I nodded toward the girl.

He glanced at her. "Bolero?"

"I think so."

"All right. Let's hear it."

I sat and began to play.

The girl stopped and lowered her flute, smiling at me. Long auburn hair curled below her shoulders. Her brown eyes were deep, with a hint of mystery about them, as if they hid a special secret.

Mr. Landers motioned for her to continue playing.

She positioned the flute to her lips and picked up where she'd left off. Soon, we were synced together.

Mr. Landers dropped into his chair, leaned back, and closed his eyes.

Halfway through the piece, I stopped.

He sat up. "What's wrong?"

"I have to catch my bus," I said.

"Where do you live?"

"On Dillon Road. About twelve miles out of town."

"Do you know any more songs?"

"Just a couple."

He glanced at the clock. "I'll drive you home at five. Dolly," he said, "do you have *Sentimental Journey* there?"

She flipped through her sheet music. "Yes, sir."

"Do you know that one?" he asked me.

"Maybe. If Dolly Anna will start it, I'll try to pick it up."

She stared at me for a moment, then smiled.

*Yes, I know your middle name, Dolly Anna Dubois.*

She spread the two sheets out on her music stand and began.

*I do remember this one.*

I picked up her place in the song.

After a moment, she came to stand beside the piano, still playing her flute.

I began to sing.

At the end, Dolly and I stared at each other.

*Two years. She'll be dead in two years! Suicide. Can I stop her? If I do, will it change the future? Of course it will. Any change I make changes the future for everyone. The blue doctor wants me to prevent global warming. That'll change the future, big time. Saving one life won't even be noticed fifty years from now.*

Dolly smiled.

*She's beautiful, and talented. No wonder I fell for her.*

"You've had voice training."

"W-what?" Mr. Landers pulled me back from wherever I was.

"You sing like a professional," he said. "You've had training."

"No. It just comes naturally."

"Do you want to transfer from one of your other classes to my music class?"

I glanced at Dolly. She gave me a hopeful smile.

"I don't know. Maybe."

"I have to go," Dolly said.

"Yes," Mr. Landers said. "And I've got to take Charley home. Can I drop you off, Dolly?"

"I'll get my books."

She took apart her flute, placed it in the case, and hurried toward her locker.

* * * * *

I sat at the kitchen table, cutting the bib from my overalls.

"Mom, can you sew belt loops on these?" I held up the remains of my overalls.

"I guess so. Why?"

"I want to wear a belt."

"Okay. Why?"

"I'm just tired of overalls."

"It's those kids at school." She brought her sewing box to the table. "They're teasing you about your clothes."

"Yeah, that and basketball."

"You're playing basketball?"

I nodded and started cutting another pair of overalls.

45

"You're butchering those. Give them to me. What do the other players wear?"

"Gym shorts."

"Vern!" she said over her shoulder.

"Yeah?" Dad answered from the living room.

"I need your leather belt, that brown one."

A few moments later, he came in with his belt. "I think he's too big for this kind of punishment." He grinned at me.

"Maybe," Mom said. "Next time you sell a load of wood, buy your athlete son some gym shorts."

"Ha, that'll be the day."

"Come on, Dad. I'll help you and Uncle Leo split firewood all weekend."

"How much are the shorts? And why do you need them?"

"I saw some in the Sears, Roebuck catalogue for a dollar-nineteen," I said. "They're for basketball."

"You're playing basketball?"

"I'm trying to learn."

"Hmm...what's your waist size?"

"Twenty-seven."

* * * * *

When I got home from school on Wednesday, I found white gym shorts and a pair of black tennis shoes on the kitchen table.

"Wow, shoes, too. Thank you, Mom."

She sat at the table, snapping green beans. She smiled. "You better thank Dad for those. Go try them on. I want to see how you look."

I was back in a few minutes, wearing my new clothes, along with a white tee shirt.

"Now you look like an athlete."

"Really?" I wadded a dishtowel and took a jump shot toward the kitchen sink. "Two points."

"I can't believe you're doing sports."

"'Bout time, right?" I asked.

"Yes, it is."

* * * * *

Late on Friday afternoon, my brother James met me as I ran back from the barn.

"Come on." He grabbed my arm. "I've got to talk to you."

*Uh-oh. Did he find out about the iPad? I know it's well-hidden under the hay, but someone could have stumbled onto it.*

"What's wrong?" I asked.

He pulled me into the barn, then dropped down on a bail of alfalfa, lying back. "They're fighting again."

"Who?"

"Mom and Dad."

"Oh." This was a regular occurrence, and James tried to keep me from seeing them whenever they were mad at each other. "Money?"

He nodded. "Mom wants to pay the electric bill, and he wants to buy a used clutch plate for the truck."

"We have the coal oil lamps."

"Yeah, but Mom likes to iron clothes and listen to her radio shows."

"But Dad needs the truck to haul wood."

"I know."

"How much is the electric bill?"

"Almost three dollars."

*Holy crap, we don't even have three dollars to pay*

47

*a bill? That's pathetic. They should've sent my guitar
instead of that iPad. I could make some serious money
with that.*

*No, dang it, it's electric; I'd need an amp.*

*I wonder where I can find an acoustic guitar. It
wouldn't sound as good, but I could pay the electric bill in
a heartbeat and buy Dad some truck parts. A fourteen-
year-old playing "American Pie." How cool would that be?*

*I wish I knew someone who could sing.*

*How can I make money with the iPad?*

* * * * *

I asked Mrs. Baker, my algebra teacher, if I could transfer
to music.

"You need to pass algebra to go on to tenth grade
next year."

"I'll still do your homework assignments and take
all the exams."

"If you think you can pass the exams, it'll be okay
with me, but you have to get permission from the
principal."

Mr. Landers talked to the principal, who approved
my transfer.

In my first music class, Mr. Landers played *You're
Nobody Till Somebody Loves You* on the guitar.

I sat on the piano bench, watching. When he
finished, I asked, "Is it hard to learn?"

"No, it just takes practice."

"You don't even look at your fingers while you
play."

"After playing for thirty years, they just know what
to do."

*True that.*

"I saw you pressing different strings with your left hand," I said.

"Those are chords, same as you do on the piano."

"You think I could learn?"

"Of course."

"Can I try?"

"Sure."

He stood and motioned for me to take the chair. I sat and took the guitar.

*Ah, this feels so good. Just like old times–or maybe future times.*

Mr. Landers positioned the fingers of my left hand on the strings. "Press these three down."

*Wow, I've got to work up some serious calluses on those fingertips.*

"Now, strum the strings with your right thumb." I did as he said, making a sweet sound with the D chord. I noticed Dolly watching me from across the room. I smiled, bringing a smile to her face.

He moved my fingers. "This is the A chord."

I strummed the strings.

"Now, do D, followed by A, then D again."

I did as he said.

"All right. This is the F chord. Four fingers."

That was difficult at first, but I got it right on the third try.

"Do A, D, F, then A again."

I flubbed it up twice on purpose, then did a little better.

"Good job."

# Chapter Six

My three oldest brothers were out of high school. D.L. was three years older than I was, but he was still a sophomore, having failed to pass the year before. With his slow progress, we might both be seniors at the same time.

Vern Jr., the oldest, worked at a sawmill in Fordland. James, next to the oldest, worked on a dairy farm, and Wayne, five years older than me, worked in a hardware store.

James was making payments on a '39 Pontiac, which left him only enough money to buy gasoline. Vern Jr. and Wayne were saving up for a down payment on cars of their own.

On the weekends all five of us helped cut firewood for Dad to sell, and in the fall we picked up black walnuts.

One good thing about having five sons is that you have a crew of captive workers. And Dad and Uncle Leo *did* put us to work, gathering walnuts on the halves. Which meant they'd find someone with a grove of black walnut trees and offer to gather the nuts for half the harvest. This scheme worked so well, we soon had a giant pile of walnuts in the back yard. Dad could sell them in Springfield for three cents a pound, but if we removed the outer hulls, he could get four cents a pound. Removing the hulls was difficult to do by hand and left a black stain on everyone's hands and clothing even lye soap couldn't remove.

While Mom and us boys hulled the walnuts by hand, Leo and Dad worked on a gimmick to automate the job. They jacked up the back of the truck until the wheels were off the ground, then built a trough from split walnut logs and slipped it under one of the rear wheels, with the front end of the trough elevated.

With the motor running and truck in low gear, the wheel spun just two inches above the bed of the trough. They then fed unhulled walnuts into the trough, and as the nuts rolled down to the spinning tire, it caught them, tearing off the hulls and spitting clean walnuts out the back. This worked so well, we soon had a truckload of hulled walnuts to take to the Hammons Walnut Company buyer in Springfield.

Dad and Leo were ecstatic when they returned home in the evening with $21.50. And that was after paying $2.60 for twenty-one gallons of gas for the truck.

Early the next morning, we were out collecting more walnuts.

* * * * *

Chicken-fried steak for supper. God, my mom could cook. It's a wonder we weren't all fat roly-polies. D.L. was a bit chubby, but the others, all lean and strong.

I never realized how poor we were when I was a kid. Mom had to make our shirts and her dresses out of feed sacks. They fit really good, and they were colorful. The Purina Feed Company printed all kinds of nice patterns on their chicken feed and flour sacks.

We got new overalls once a year from the Sears, Roebuck catalog. Well, the older boys got new ones; all my clothes were hand-me-downs.

Dad and Leo didn't make much money; three dollars for a rick of wood, when they could sell it.

All our food, except for sugar, salt, and flour, came

from the farm. We had over forty acres in corn, milo, and wheat. Four milk cows, two mean bulls, twenty-five pigs, two dumb mules, ten turkeys, twelve geese, and I don't know how many chickens. I loved those goose eggs. Scramble one of those, and you had a whole breakfast.

Mom and Dad didn't actually own the farm. The house and land were rented from Buster Moore, at twenty-three dollars a month.

* * * * *

It was quiet around the supper table. We knew better than to talk when Mom and Dad were fighting.

"Right after supper," Mom said, "I want you two boys to get your homework done." She looked from me to D.L.

"D.L.," Dad said. "Not much firewood in here."

"Nobody split the firewood," D.L. said.

"Vern Jr.?" Dad asked.

"It's James's turn this week," Vern Jr. said.

"There's no firewood to split, Dad," James said. "You took all of it to Fordland."

Dad glanced at the stove, then at the wood box. We followed his eyes.

"Looks like enough wood for breakfast, Avice."

Oh, chilly. And he called her 'Avice' instead of 'Mom,' like he usually did.

She only nodded as she sipped her coffee.

"I hate homework," D.L. said.

"I'll help you," I said.

Wayne laughed, then the others, too. That's what I was going for; lighten things up a little.

D.L. sneered at me and pushed his corn around his plate.

52

* * * * *

After supper, James and I washed dishes.

Everyone helped with the kitchen cleanup, except Dad, who went to the living room with Uncle Leo to listen to the news on the radio.

After the table was wiped down, D.L. and I spread out our homework, while the three older boys went to the front room. Mom sat at the table, peeling potatoes.

I finished my algebra assignment, then read three chapters in my history textbook. Medieval Europe. The fall of the Roman Empire, the rise of Islam, the Crusades...all very interesting. Twenty minutes later, I went to the front room to listen to the news, leaving Mom to watch over D.L. as he struggled with geometry.

* * * * *

That night, after I was sure everyone was asleep; I slipped out to the barn.

I lit the lantern in the loft.

On the iPad, I read about wind turbines and lithium-ion batteries.

They wouldn't be invented until the 1970s, but I found the patent information with the original design specs. I also read the latest discoveries and updated specifications for the batteries, making them smaller and much more efficient.

I opened the other boxes that came with my iPad. One was the solar panels I'd have to set up to recharge the computer. I was surprised to find a printer in the third box.

They'd even sent some copier paper with it. I plugged the printer into the USB port and tried it out by printing a page of sheet music. It was a small printer, and I had to feed single sheets of paper by hand, but it worked perfectly.

*This'll really speed things up.*

The solar panels came with a tube of adhesive, a 110 volt inverter, and wiring to connect to the power input on the iPad. The printer battery would charge through the USB port.

I read the instructions for the solar panels, then climbed out through the hayloft door and onto the pulley beam. After tossing the panels onto the roof, I gripped the edge to pull myself up.

It was after midnight, and with no moon, it was quite dark. The roof was steep, but with my bare feet braced on the cedar shake shingles, I could keep myself from sliding off.

My eyes slowly adjusted to the darkness as I unfolded the panels. I spread the tube of adhesive as instructed, then pressed the panels onto the sticky glue. With the end of the wire in my teeth, I worked my way back down through the hayloft door. I plugged the adapter into the iPad. Tomorrow, after a few hours of sunshine, I'd see if the charging system worked.

With the panel installed on the back side of the barn roof, no one would notice it.

Before I climbed down the ladder, I decided to print out two more items.

* * * * *

At breakfast, I sketched a few lines on one of the line drawings I'd printed out the night before, pretending to have drawn it myself.

"What'cha got there, Charley Eye?" James asked as

he took a bite of scrambled eggs.

I slid the diagram over to him.

"Wow! What a car," James said.

"Let me see," Vern Jr. said.

James pushed it over to him.

"Beautiful. What model is it?"

"I think I'll call it a Mustang." It was a detailed drawing of the first Ford Mustang, built in 1964. "It'll run on electricity instead of gasoline."

Dad reached for the drawing. He studied it for a moment. "Won't work."

"Why?" I asked.

"The batteries will be so heavy, the car won't be able to move."

"Lithium-ion batteries, Dad. They're small, lightweight, and store a lot of power. Eighty-five pounds of lithium batteries will provide more power than fifteen hundred pounds of lead-acid batteries."

"And you know this because...?"

"Science books."

"Oh, yeah," he said. "You've been reading a lot lately."

I nodded.

*Maybe I'm moving too fast. I don't want to freak everyone out.*

"You forgot the headlights," Dad said.

"They're concealed. See these panels, here? When you switch the lights on, the panels flip up, lifting the headlights into place."

"Neat-o," James said.

Dad reached across the table to take the other drawing I'd 'finished.' "Fancy windmill."

"Actually, it's a wind turbine, to generate electricity."

Mom leaned toward Dad to see the drawing. "How'd you come up with that?"

"I...um...I found it in—"

Dad interrupted me. "Yes, we know. You read about it in a science book at school." He studied the drawing for a moment. "Will it work?"

"We'll have to build one to find out."

.

# Chapter Seven

I remember always hating church. It was so boring. But now I loved it. I loved everything.

*Living my life over. What could be sweeter? Until my lights go out.*

"Why are we going to church on Wednesday, Mom?" I asked.

"Funeral."

"Oh, no. Who died?"

"Mrs. Latchcroft."

"Aw, I liked Mrs. Latchcroft. She made fried pies."

"Yes, she did."

We wore our Sunday clothes and good shoes. Lots of people were there, maybe fifty or more. It was very solemn.

The preacher spoke for a long time, then Mr. William Latchcroft went up to the front and tried to say how much he loved his wife and how he'd miss her, but he couldn't get many words out without breaking down. Soon, his daughter went up, took him by the arm, and led him back to his seat.

A lady then went to the front and said how well Mrs. Latchcroft could make quilts.

When she sat down, the preacher asked if anyone

else would like to say anything.

I raised my hand.

Dad gave me a hard look, but I kept my hand up.

The preacher stared at me for a minute, then nodded to me.

I stood. "Mrs. Latchcroft made really good fried pies."

A few people giggled, then put their fingers to their lips.

Monica, a girl in the eighth grade at Dillon School, sat a few rows in front of us. She nodded in agreement, then smiled at me.

Before anyone else had a chance to speak, I began to sing. This was either going to get me into big trouble, or it would knock their socks off. I really didn't know which.

"Amazing grace, how sweet the sound..." Most people were teary-eyed before I started, so this should be easy. I raised my voice. "...that saved a wretch like me."

As I sang, a few people stared in stunned reaction, then some sniffled and a few smiled.

I put a little vibrato in my voice, then added some riffs.

"I once was lost, but now am found."

A woman wiped her eyes.

"T'was blind, but now I see."

More women began to cry, my mom included. Even old man Latchcroft pulled out his handkerchief.

*Yeah, this is an easy audience. Sure wish I had a guitar.*

By the end of the song, most of the people were in tears.

After the preacher ended the service, people came to hug me, and some shook my hand.

"That was the most beautiful thing I've ever heard

in my life," Mrs. Moore said after she hugged me.

"Thank you, Mrs. Moore."

"Like an angel," a lady said. "Just like a sweet singing angel."

*That's what I was going for.*

"Thank you, ma'am."

Mr. Latchcroft, still with wet cheeks, took my hand in his big, rough one. "That was just..." He sniffed and swallowed. "I can't..." He wiped his face. "Linda would have loved...to hear it."

"Thank you, sir."

Monica shook my hand and squeezed it a little.

Next came the preacher. "When did you learn to sing like that?"

"Here," I said, "in church."

"Well, I never knew you were listening. I'm proud of you, son."

I shook his hand.

* * * * *

In the front seat of the truck, I sat between Mom and Dad. The other boys had to ride in the back.

"First wind turbines, now singing like a nightingale," Dad said. "What the heck?"

"I don't know," Mom said. "And it happened overnight."

"What else can you do, Charley Eye?" Dad asked.

"I can carve a whistle from a willow stick, like you showed me with your Barlow knife."

Dad pushed the starter button with his foot. "But what else that we don't know about?" The old truck coughed to life.

"I think that's all, Dad."

# Chapter Eight

I knew in 1945, Mom and Dad were less than a year from their breakup. Soon after the divorce, my two older brothers, Vern Jr. and James, would go live with Dad. They'd eventually end up in California, with their stepmother, Marie. Mom would move the three remaining boys in with her parents in Oklahoma and start waitressing in cafés to support me, D.L., and Wayne.

Our nuclear family was about to explode, injuring all of us in one way or another. Some more than others.

My instructions said I had to save the world, but first I had to save the family. For that, I needed a guitar.

On Friday after music class, I asked Mr. Landers if I could borrow the guitar for the weekend.

"Sure. Practice on those chords, and on Monday we'll work on something new."

* * * * *

"Where'd you get the guitar, son?" Dad asked when I came in from school.

"Mr. Landers, our music teacher, taught me some chords and told me to practice over the weekend."

After supper, I strummed the guitar, playing all the chords. I was itching to start playing real music, but I kept it slow and probably irritated everyone with the endless repetition.

I went out on the back porch to practice. It was

driving me nuts, too, but they had to think I was just learning to play. I couldn't suddenly master the *Flight of the Bumblebee*. Which reminded me, I had to let the fingernails on my right hand grow longer.

* * * * *

On Tuesday afternoon, Coach Jameson asked me if I'd ever played football.

"Yes, sir."

"Where?"

Vietnam, I wanted to tell him. The 2nd Battalion of the 6th Marine Regiment, stationed at Da Nang, had the best football team in South Vietnam. We played every Sunday afternoon unless a good game was on TV or we were on patrol. The teams were even reluctant to leave the field when we came under mortar attack.

We weren't number one because we played a nice, friendly game. We had no rules, no padding, and no referees. The staff sergeant who kept score also watched the time. He told us when to take a beer break at halftime and when the game was over. We didn't score many touchdowns, but we had plenty of fistfights, resulting in bloody noses, black eyes, and missing teeth. This wasn't a big deal to us. When we went out on patrol or came under attack, death and bloody wounds were our constant companions.

The Army's 101st Airborne's team came to our base to take us on, wearing their military helmets. We laughed them off the field. They tossed their helmets aside and came back out, ready for a good brawl. And we gave it to them. We also beat the hell out of them two years running.

"In our backyard," I said to Coach, "with my four brothers."

61

"All right, let's see what you can do."

He made us wear leather helmets, but no other protection.

Crammer thought he was a quarterback, but after I sacked him for the third time, he complained to the coach.

"He's not playing fair, Coach."

"Charley didn't break any rules. If your boys can't protect you, you'll get sacked."

"All right…" Crammer tossed the football to me. "Let's see *him* quarterback."

We had two good receivers. I threw a few short passes, right into their arms.

On our third play, I threw a pretty thirty-yard spiral.

Crammer blindsided me after the ball was already in the receiver's hands.

I went down hard, with him on top of me. After shoving him off, I stood, then pretended to slip on the grass. I fell with my knee in his gut. He didn't get up for awhile.

We ran a few more plays, while Crammer sat on the bench, staring daggers at me.

"Okay, boys," Coach said. "Hit the showers. Good work, Charley. You want to play next Saturday, against Marshfield?"

"I wish I could, Coach, but I have to help my dad cut wood."

"All right, maybe later in the year."

"Yeah, I'd like that."

He patted my shoulder. "See you tomorrow."

* * * * *

Two weeks later, Mom and Dad threw a birthday party for

our neighbor, Buster Moore. It was a Friday night, and I'd brought the guitar home, as usual.

After dinner, all the men sat in the living room, smoking. They also passed around a jar of bootleg whiskey.

My brothers and I played Monopoly at the kitchen table, while the four ladies sat at the table with us, sewing and gossiping.

"Hey, Charley Eye," James said, "play some music."

*Finally!*

"I don't know about that," I said. "I'm not very good."

"Yeah, you are," Wayne said. "Play that one about the dragon."

"Well, all right."

I strummed the strings a few times, then played and sang, *Puff, the Magic Dragon.*

Halfway through, I noticed everyone in the front room had gone quiet.

After *Puff*, I began *Scarborough Fair.*

Dad and some of the other men came into the kitchen, standing just inside the door.

"Come out here," Buster said from the living room, "so we can hear."

I continued to play as I went into the room and stood by the stove. When I finished, everyone clapped their hands.

"Where did you learn that?" Mom asked.

"Music class."

"You got any more like that?" Buster asked.

"Umm...let me think."

*I'd better keep it slow and easy for now. These old-timers really wouldn't appreciate rock 'n roll.*

I played and sang *Sentimental Journey*, then *You Are My Sunshine*, followed by *This Land is Your Land.*

That one got them singing along.

By the end of the evening, everyone was having a good time. Of course, the men were just a bit drunk, but that was okay; I was on my way.

"Why don't you play at the box supper?" Mrs. Moore asked. "It's next Saturday night."

*Heck, yeah!*

I glanced at Mom.

"What do you think, Dad?" Mom asked.

"I'll drink to that." And he did.

The other men laughed and followed suit. The quart fruit jar was soon empty.

* * * * *

Borrowing the guitar from music class was okay for the weekends, but I really needed one of my own. I couldn't ask my parents to buy one; we had no money, not yet anyway. So, I'd have to show them I could make money with it.

Dad had tried many different professions, mastering none. I don't know if it was because he didn't stick to a job long enough to learn the skills required for advancement or he just got bored. I think it was the latter. He wanted to move on and start making big money.

If his fourteen-year-old son could play music like an experienced troubadour, Dad would recognize the monetary potential. And I had thirty years' experience playing beer joints and roadhouses from Oklahoma to Germany to Saigon to Alaska. Give me a smoky dive and a stage, and I'd be in my element. And if that joint had a pool table, I could make a few bucks at eight-ball, too.

In the loft of the round barn, I munched my peanut butter and jelly sandwich and browsed Wikipedia, reading about health risks in the 1940s. There were many, and I was appalled by the lack of knowledge about simple hygiene. Even the daily brushing of one's teeth was almost unheard of, not to mention the avoidance of spoiled food or unclean eating utensils. And who knows what lurked in the drinking water?

*My God, these people are almost primitive.*

Inoculations against contagious diseases were few and practically unknown in the outback of the Missouri Ozark Mountains.

In looking through the thousands of books they'd loaded onto the iPad for me, I was pleased to find eighteen of my novels, including the one about Hannibal. I wished I could print that out and show it to Mrs. Adams, my history teach—

"Charley Eye! Where are you?"

*Mom! Oh, my God! She can't catch me up here with this.*

I switched off the computer, put it back in the box, and covered it with hay.

"Coming, Mom." I ran for the ladder.

"What are you doing up there?"

"I was just...um..."

"James said he couldn't find you to help with the firewood."

"Yes, I remember..." I climbed down the ladder.

"Have you been up there in the hay loft all day?"

"Not all day."

She folded her arms and stared at me, trying very hard to be angry.

I hugged her. "I love you, Mom."

She pushed me out at arm's length, and looked up at me; I was a couple of inches taller than she was. "You've been acting very strange for the last six weeks."

I nodded, but I knew I had her at "I love you."

"James said that electric car you drew might actually work."

"Maybe." I looked down at my bare toes, making circles in the dirt.

She pulled me into a hug. "You have a gift, and I just don't know what to do with it."

I wanted to tell her the gift was the mind and experience of a man who was much older than she was, but instead I said, "If I really have anything of value, Mom, it's for you."

* * * * *

In music class on Monday, I played the guitar and sang *Galveston*.

Several students and two teachers squeezed into the room to listen.

"Where did that come from?" Mr. Landers asked after I finished the song.

"My neighbor loaned me some sheet music over the weekend. What do you think of it?"

"I've never heard it before, but it's great."

The next day, I performed *San Francisco*.

On Wednesday, Mr. Landers moved the music class to the cafeteria, so more students and teachers could listen.

Dolly and I performed *Amazing Grace* and *I Love a Rainy Night*.

Someone asked for *Puff, The Magic Dragon*, so we did that one, followed by *Country Roads*.

After a couple more familiar songs, we got a nice round of applause.

*We really need a drummer.*

* * * * *

In science class, Mr. Flanders talked about an upcoming event.

"The science fair is only six weeks away. I think it's important to stretch our imaginations by constructing visual displays. I will randomly select students for two-person teams. You will work together to produce a model of cutting-edge developments in science."

I took out a sheet of paper and began a sketch.

Mr. Flanders paced the aisle of the classroom, his hands clasped behind his back. "This year, I would like *not* to see another working model of a coal mine or a volcano spewing bread dough and baking soda. Give me something new, refreshing, imaginative." He turned at the back of the room and walked between the desks. "During the war, many things were invented out of necessity. Devices we needed to defeat our enemies. Now..."

He paused beside my desk. I knew he was there, but I continued to draw the object that would be discovered in the very near future.He walked on.

"Now I want to see things or ideas that will improve the human condition. Expand the horizons of discovery."At the front of the room, he turned to face us. "There will be medals awarded for first, second, and third place. Plus honorable mention for the next three runners-up." He reached for a sheet of paper on his desk. "Here are the parings; Fanny Ross and Owen Brown, Ryan Foster and Wanda Hoffman, Patsy McCarthy and Justin Crammer, Ember Coldstream and Charley Brindley..."

I glanced at Ember to find her smiling at me.

"Melody Sandoval and Matthew Russell..."

Crammer gave Patsy an ugly sneer. She looked at me with a helpless expression. I smiled and mouthed the words, "I wish we could trade partners." She nodded in agreement.

"Give this project some thought," Mr. Flanders said, "because it will count for 25 percent of your final grade in this class."

* * * * *

After class, Ember stopped me in the hall.

"What are we going to do for the project?" she asked.

"A model of DNA."

"What's DNA?"

"Deoxyribonucleic acid."

She looked blank. "What's deoxlec...?"

"It's the microscopic material present in all living organisms, the main constituent of chromosomes."

"What's a chromosome?"

I exhaled through my nose. "I'll finish drawing the model tonight and show it to you tomorrow."

"Why can't we grow bean sprouts under glass?"

"Too easy."

"Build a model of the solar system?"

"That's been done."

"How about a clay model of a Neandertal guy dragging his girl by the hair?"

"It's Neander*thal*, and that business about dragging women by the hair is nothing but a myth."

"All right," she said. "DNA. What do you want me to do?"

"I don't want you to do anything. Just stay out of my way."

"Mr. Flanders said we have to work together on the project. I don't like us being paired any more than you do,

68

but I don't want to flunk science."

"Just go hang out with your boyfriend and leave me alone."

"I don't have a boyfriend."

"What about Crammer?" I asked.

She scoffed. "Crammer? The fat-headed jock? I can't stand him."

"Why do you spend so much time with him?"

"Are you spying on me?" Ember asked.

The bell rang for the next class.

"You're a complete idiot," I said. "You know that?"

She looked down at the floor and slipped her hands behind herself. "I don't think I'm complete..." She looked up at me, her eyes moist. "...yet."

*Remember, this is Ember. She's playing me.*

"All right. We'll need a Tinker Toy set and six colors of paint."

"Tinker Toys, really?"

I nodded. "I have to go to history."

She grabbed my arm.

"What?"

"Paint brushes?"

"Yeah, unless you're going to finger-paint the Tinker Toys."

She smiled. "What songs are you playing today in the cafeteria?"

"I don't know yet."

"How about *Sweet Home Alabama* and *Country Roads*?"

"I'm tired of those two." I saw Patsy beside my locker, waiting. "Gotta go."

"My God," Patsy said as I approached. "Did he do this to us on purpose?"

"Mr. Flanders?" I asked. "I doubt he's aware of

which of us are friends and which are enemies."

"Well, he sure paired up some enemies."

"Yes, he did. Where's Melody?"

"She said she'd see us in history."

* * * * *

The forty-five minute music class in the cafeteria had become a more of a mini concert than any teaching. Some of the kids cut class to listen to the music, while a few teachers joined their students in the cafeteria.

I glanced at Ember where she stood in the back of the room, then I played *Sweet Home Alabama*, followed by *Country Roads*.

That brought a smile to her face.

* * * * *

On Monday, Patsy wasn't in history. After class, I asked Melody if she knew where she was.

"She had a doctor's appointment today."

"Ah," I said. *Good. Maybe it's about hypothyroidism.* "I hope she's all right." We walked toward our next class.

"It's just a check-up."

"Okay."

"Do they have a set of drums in the music room?" Melody asked.

"Yeah." I stopped and reached for her arm. "Why do you ask?"

"My brother played drums. When I was little, I always begged him to let me play. By the time I was six, he got tired of me pestering him, so he taught me how."

"Really?" We walked on.

70

"When he joined the army in '42 and went to North Africa, I had the drums all to myself."

"Can you meet me in the music room after classes?"

"Sure." She looked up at me and smiled.

I returned her smile. "I'd like to hear you play."

After music class, I asked Mr. Landers if he'd mind if Melody played the drums for a few minutes after school.

"I've never known a girl to play drums," he said.

"Me either."

* * * * *

I waited for Melody outside her English classroom, her last class of the day.

We hurried to the music room, where we found Mr. Landers. Dolly was there, too, practicing on her flute.

I introduced Melody to both of them.

Mr. Landers shook her hand, but Dolly gave her an icy hello.

"I have to catch my bus pretty soon," Melody said.

"Okay," I said. "Just do five minutes on the drums, of whatever you like."

She sat at the drums, placed her foot on the pedal for the base drum, adjusted the cymbal stand closer to her, then played a roll across all five drums. I think she just wanted to get a feel for the sound.

She then began to play.

It was amazing.

Mr. Landers leaned toward me and whispered, "Do you know what that is?"

"I have no idea," I whispered.

"That's a Gene Krupa piece from *Song of India*."

She ended with a quick boogie beat, then a few quick taps on the symbol. She touched the symbol to

71

silence it as she looked at us.

Mr. Landers and I applauded.

Dolly pulled apart her flute, shoved it into her case, and slammed the lid. "I have to go, Mr. Landers."

"Okay," he said. "See you tomorrow."

"Bye, Dolly," I said.

The door swished open, and she was gone.

"I have to catch my bus," Melody said.

"I'll go with you," I said. "Thank you, Mr. Landers."

"Melody," Mr. Landers said, "I need to talk to you tomorrow."

"Okay, Mr. Landers."

Outside in the hall, I held out my fist for her to bump. "That was beautiful."

"Really?" She bumped my fist.

* * * * *

During the next music class in the cafeteria, Melody backed me up on the drums, and she did a great job.

We played *Dancing Queen*, then *My Special Angel*.

Even on the songs Melody hadn't heard before, she picked up the beat, and added some quiet drum rolls when I paused between lines of singing.

* * * * *

Ember brought a Tinker Toy set and six small bottles of model aircraft paint, along with brushes to the study hall where we worked on the project. I had a paper bag with a hundred small wooden balls I'd bought at the TG&Y Five and Dime store. They had holes drilled through them and fit nicely on the ends of the Tinker Toy sticks.

"Scientists believe DNA has a double helix

structure," I said.

"What's a helix?" Ember asked.

"It's like a twisted ladder."

"What's a—"

I interrupted her. "A double helix is two helixes spiraling together."

"Oh."

"We need an equal number of red, blue, green, yellow, and white balls," I said.

She opened the bottle of red paint and started on the first ball. "I'm getting paint on my fingers."

"If you put the ball on the end of one of the Tinker Toy sticks, you can paint it without touching it."

"Ha, good idea. What's DNA got to with us, anyway?"

"You'll need to paint the sticks, too."

"Since I'm doing all the work, what are you going to do?"

"Build a rotating base and concealed spotlights. And also a tri-fold board for the background."

"Oh," she said.

"DNA is like a blueprint containing instructions for each person's genetic code. But it's not just in humans; it's a part of most living organisms. You could think of it as the recipe that makes us unique. Your complete DNA is called a genome, and it contains over two billion bases, twenty-two thousand genes, and twenty-three pairs of chromosomes. Genes determine things like what color your hair and eyes are. You can think of the chromosomes as packing material that holds the DNA and proteins together."

She stared at me. "What's a blueprint?"

"Okay...the sticks should be green, yellow, and blue."

* * * * *

I made an 'A' on my six-weeks algebra exam, without even cracking the book. That made Mrs. Baker happy.

At Melody's house, after we worked on our homework, I played the guitar, while she played her brother's drums.

I'd made three copies of *Sister Golden Hair*. Patsy read the words from her copy as Melody and I played and I sang.

After the third time through the song, Melody had the drumbeats down perfectly. When we started again from the beginning, Patsy sang with me.

* * * * *

During the box supper, I played *As Time Goes By* and *Don't Sit Under The Apple Tree*.

My fingertips were beginning to callus, which really made the playing easier. I'd also allowed the nails on my right hand to grow longer.

At the end of the night, I asked Mrs. Caldwell if we could use Dillon School on the next Saturday night for a little concert. She said it would be fine as long as we swept up after the show and helped pay the electric bill.

Mom and Mrs. Moore passed the word around the neighborhood.

On Saturday night, we had eight adults, plus ten children.

I started off with *Puff the Magic Dragon* for the kids, then *If You're Happy And You Know It*, and *This Old Man*.

As I played *He's Got the Whole World in His*

74

*Hands*, followed by *If I Had a Hammer*, I noticed a few more adults come in. As I played *Galveston*, I counted fifteen adults.

*That's a pretty nice-sized audience, for a start.*

After *Galveston*, I asked for requests.

The kids wanted to hear *Puff the Magic Dragon* again, and a lady asked for *Scarborough Fair*.

That night at supper, we talked about the performance. Mom said several people asked about the next show and she told them I might do another one on the next Saturday night.

"Is that okay?" she asked me.

"Sure."

* * * * *

On the next Saturday night, the audience had grown to twenty, plus my mom and dad. He wasn't bashful at all about passing around his hat for a few coins. And the people didn't mind paying; entertainment was pretty thin in the 1940s Ozark Mountains.

That evening at dinner, Dad counted out $3.46 in change he'd collected.

Mom took the money and dropped it into a Bell jar. "That's more than enough for next month's electric bill, Charley Eye. You've done good."

"Thank you, Mom. I love this spaghetti."

* * * * *

Ember and I worked on our DNA project in the science classroom. I'd constructed a tri-fold background and painted it white. It measured six feet across and three feet high. It was laid flat on the floor so she could use her nice penmanship to letter the information I'd collected from my iPad.

The other kids were working on their projects in the cafeteria. Ryan Foster and Wanda Hoffman worked on fingerprint analysis, while Patsy and Justin Crammer worked on a clay model of a Neanderthal couple.

While Ember lay on her stomach, working on the lettering on the background, I assembled a round base with a spiral spring underneath. Like a watch, when it was wound up and released, it would rotate slowly for almost an hour before needing to be wound again.

"Can we set this thing up somewhere?" Amber asked. "It's really hard to work on the floor."

"Sure. Where do you want it?"

She pulled three desks together. "How's that?"

I move the background to the desks and positioned the three sections so it would stand up. It was shaky, but she could sit or kneel in the seats to work.

"This is much better." She adjusted her skirt and began lettering the center section.

The wooden background was now between her and the door. I sat on the floor behind her. I'd put together two small electric lights to illuminate the model from the sides as it turned.

"Can you help me move this over?" Ember asked.

"Sure."

I lifted the background and moved it to the side.

"A little more this way." She reached to place her hand on mine.

"H-how's that?" I glanced at her to see a sweet smile.

"Very..." She leaned toward me and licked her lips. "Nice."

I swallowed. "Yes, it's very nice."

I leaned toward her. Our lips were on a slow collision course. Danger signs popped up all over the inside of my head. Stop signs, dangerous curve ahead, railroad crossing, STOP SIGNS. But I saw nothing but those beautiful blue eyes and wet lips.

She closed the last few inches and kissed me.

I'd never felt anything like that before. My whole body reacted. All the danger signs in the world couldn't keep me from taking her in my arms.

She glanced up at the clock, then wrapped her arms around me, kissing me again.

I felt her tongue brush my lips as she reached down to unbuckle my belt and unzip my pants.

She unbuttoned my shirt and pressed herself to me. I could feel her warm breasts heaving against my bare chest. She pushed down my pants.

Even the clicking of the door handle couldn't stop me.

Ember suddenly ripped open her blouse, popping off the buttons. She yanked up her bra, and as she did, she hit the background with her elbow, knocking it to the floor.

"What in the world?!"

I jerked around to see Mr. Flanders standing in the doorway. And behind him, looking over his shoulders, were Patsy, Melody, and Crammer.

Ember slapped me so hard, I stumbled backward and almost fell, with my pants down around my ankles.

"He attacked me!" She jerked her bra back in place and pulled her blouse closed. She ran to Mr. Flanders. "Get him away from me."

Crammer came at me before I could get my pants up.

He slugged me in the side of my head, sending me onto a desk, then to the floor.

"My God!" Patsy said. "What have you done?"

"Crammer!" Mr. Flanders said. "Get Ember out of here. You girls, too. Go on, get out of here."

Ember was in hysterics as Crammer led her out and closed the door.

* * * * *

I sat in Mr. Nelson's office. He was the principal. Mr. Flanders and Mr. Coldstream, Ember's father, were there. No one said anything.

Mr. Nelson's secretary knocked and entered. "They're on their way," she said.

"Thank you, Miss Johnson," Mr. Nelson said.

I didn't know who was on their way; probably Ember's mother and the police. I was in big trouble, and I had no defense. I could apologize to her parents, to Mr. Flanders, and to Ember, but I had no excuse for what I did. And the police certainly wouldn't care about any excuses. In Missouri in the 1940s, sex wasn't even discussed, let alone performed before marriage. If young people were ever caught in the act, they'd most probably be forced into a quick shotgun wedding. It simply wasn't done, at least not in a classroom.

Soon, we heard another knock on the door. I hoped for the police instead of Ember's mother.

I was somewhat relieved when two city policemen came into the room.

"You're Charley Eye?" one of the officers asked. "The singer on the radio?"

"Yes, sir." I stood, ready to be handcuffed and led away.

"Did you rape her?" the other officer asked.

That was a shock to me, but I guess a reasonable

78

question under the circumstances.

"No, sir. I didn't."

"We were told her blouse was torn open."

"She did that."

The other cop laughed.

The first policeman glanced at him, then back at me. "And your pants were down."

"Ember did that, too."

The questioning cop shot a look at his pal before he laughed again.

"So, she ripped her blouse open and took your pants off?"

"She also shoved her bra up," I said.

Mr. Coldstream had heard enough. "This is outrageous." He jumped to his feet. "This hoodlum tried to rape my daughter. If Mr. Flanders hadn't come in, he would have. Ember was quick enough to slap him and shove him away before he could do anything more."

"Were you trying to rape her?" the officer asked.

"No, sir."

"What were you thinking?"

I looked down at the floor. "I guess I wasn't thinking. Just reacting to her actions."

"He's trying to blame my daughter for what he did."

"No, Mr. Coldstream. I take full responsibility."

*Good God, I have the mind and experience of seventy-nine years, and yet I let a fourteen-year-old trollop entrap me. I should be punished severely.*

"I saw the danger signs and chose to ignore them."

*Hormones overruled logic, but that's still no excuse. All I can do is throw myself on my sword, or, since I don't have a sword, on the mercy of someone here.*

I looked from the policemen to the principal, to Mr. Flanders, to Mr. Coldstream.

*Actually, I think I'd prefer the sword. Who's the most aggrieved? The girl's father, of course. I thought of my own future daughters and what I went through with them when they were teenagers. If I'd caught a boy having sex with one of them, I would have wanted to murder him. That's how Mr. Coldstream feels right now.*

"Mr. Coldstream," I said. "If I were in your place, I would take a swing at the face of this worthless bum, right now. Or pick up that hat tree and pound it over his head. I deserve anything you have in mind."

"You can't imagine how much I'd love to do just that."

"I understand."

I used my foot to scoot the heavy hat tree over toward him. I thought he was going to reach for it, but Mr. Flanders saved me from a severe beating.

"Can I say something?" he asked. The principal nodded to him. "I'm not going to defend Charley Eye's behavior. It's abhorrent and reprehensible."

"Yes," Mr. Coldstream said. "It certainly was."

"But I would like to point out that his performance and actions over the past two months have been nothing less than outstanding."

"That's no excuse," Mr. Coldstream said.

"No, I'm not making excuses for him. He has to be punished for his actions today. I'm just saying I think his conduct to this point has been a credit to this school. It's not just his music, but also his academic and social behavior is an asset to all of us."

"I agree, but..."

"He could be arrested, charged with attempted rape, maybe even sent to jail, but if that happens, is it the best outcome for our community?"

Mr. Coldstream looked at me, perhaps expecting

me to beg for forgiveness.

"I'm willing to take whatever punishment; corporal, capital, or jail time," I said. "Any of those you choose to impose on me. I've committed a crime, and I'll take the consequences."

Mr. Coldstream stared at me for a moment. "My daughter's reputation is at stake here. I want this criminal arrested."

"I have to agree," Mr. Nelson said. "Take him away."

"All right, let's go," the policeman said. "Are we going to have to put the cuffs on you."

"No," I said. "Mr. Flanders, would you mind driving out to my house and telling Mom I've been arrested."

"Sure, I can do that."

* * * * *

Jail cells haven't changed over the past sixty years; they're still bleak, cold, Spartan, depressing...as they should be. *Drunk and disorderly, fighting in a public eating establishment, destroying pool hall equipment, sleeping on the street, and being disrespectful to a Paris gendarme, i.e., spitting on his pretty blue uniform. And now the worst of all; attempted rape of a minor.*

"Charley Eye, what have you done?"

"Mom!" I left the bunk and went to the bars of my cell.

"What the hell?" Dad asked.

I told them the whole story.

"You're saying she trapped you?" Dad asked.

"Yes."

"You've never lied to us before—that I know of—but this sounds crazy. Why would she do that?"

81

"I don't know. And it does sounds crazy, but I've never lied to either of you."

"Vern," Mom said, "he may have turned into a minor genius and a great musician, but he's an idiot when it comes to girls. No one can learn how a woman's mind works from reading books."

"That's for damn sure," Dad said.

"Was she one of the kids who used to tease you?" Mom asked.

"Yeah. And her boyfriend, Crammer. They were the worst."

"And then, four months ago, you came out of your shell and began talking to people, playing music and sports."

I nodded. "That's true."

"They were jealous of your new popularity. That's what I think. And they just wanted to cut you down a few notches."

"You're probably right," Dad said. "Here's the deal, Charley Eye. Tomorrow morning we have to go before the judge. All you can do is tell him the same story you just told us, and throw yourself on the mercy of the court. He'll probably set a trial date, and, hopefully turn you loose until then."

"Thanks, Dad. And you, too, Mom. You're the best parents ever."

"You'll have to spend the night in jail," Mom said. "We'll pick you up in the morning to go before the judge."

* * * * *

Judge Leroy Hamilton was not happy to see me in his courtroom.

He made me stand and wait while he read the

police report and the statements from Ember and all the others.

"Attempted rape of a minor child is a serious offence," Judge Hamilton said.

"Yes, sir."

"If convicted, the sentence can be five to ten years in prison." He stared at me, apparently waiting for his words to sink in.

"I-I didn't know that, Your Honor."

"Other than your parents..." He glanced at Mom and Dad sitting behind me, "Only one other person is willing to speak on your behalf." He looked at the papers on his desk. "Mr. Flanders. I believe he's one of your teachers."

"Yes, sir. My music teacher."

"I've read Mr. Flanders' statement, along with the others, and I have to be honest with you, son. If this is all there is to this sordid tale, you're probably looking at five years in jail."

I heard Mom make a noise, like a gasp and cry together. I felt more sorry for her than for myself. "I'm resigned to my punishment, your honor."

"All right." He checked his calendar. "I'm setting your trial date twenty-three days from today, at 9 a.m. And I'm setting you free on your own recognizance. Watch our step, or you could spend the next three weeks in jail."

"Yes, sir. I'll stay out of trouble."

Outside the courthouse, Mom hugged me. "I'm just glad he let you go until the trial."

"Yeah, me, too."

"Now we have to go see your principal," Dad said.

* * * * *

"Hello, Nelson," Dad said when we were shown into the principal's office.

"Brindley," he said, then stood. "And Mrs. Brindley." He waved her to a chair.

Dad and I sat in the chairs beside her.

"It's been a long time," Dad said.

Mr. Nelson nodded and took his chair behind the huge mahogany desk. "Now, then. I'm afraid I'll have to suspend Charles from school until the trial."

"You know Debora Wilson's back?" Dad said.

Mr. Nelson lifted a shoulder, looking puzzled.

"Come on, Debby Wilson. You, her and me went to school together, right here at Fordland. Class of 1922. You and I graduated, she didn't"

"Oh, yes. I think she was that short, fat girl, from Texas."

"No, she was a pretty blonde. We saw her last month at the grocery store in Seymour. Right, Avice?"

"Yes. In high school she was a tall blonde, very popular. I was two years behind you guys. Her son was with her in the store. He's about twenty-three, same age as Vern Jr."

"Nice young man," Dad said. "We had a good conversation. The logging company in Springfield put him on as a driver. I think we'll be seeing a lot of the two of them."

"Well, I—."

Mom interrupted Mr. Nelson. "So sad about her leaving school just before graduation."

"What's your middle name, Nelson?" Dad asked.

"David. Why?"

"Interesting. That's what Debby named her son."

Mr. Nelson squirmed in his chair as he looked from Mom's smiling face to Dad's. "What do you want?"

"Oh, nothing much," Dad said. "Just no suspension from school for Charley Eye."

"And?" Mr. Nelson asked.

"That all, for now."

* * * * *

I was lucky to be allowed to attend my classes because I loved school. However, my worst punishment would came from my classmates.

I was universally shunned. Even Patsy, Melody, and Dolly would have nothing to do with me. I practiced music alone and began bringing my lunch again and eating in the deserted bleachers.

Whenever I encountered Ember in the hallways, she was always hanging onto Crammer. They sneered and told me to go back to plowing and shoveling cow shit because that's all I was good for.

During science class, Mr. Flanders asked me and Ember to come see him after school.

"I'm aware," he said when we met with him in the science room, "that you two haven't been working on your project."

"I don't actually want to be attacked again," Ember said, looking at me.

"Let me state this as clearly and succinctly as I can."

She wrinkled her brow.

"*Concisamente,*" I said.

"Oh."

"What did you say to her?" Mr. Flanders asked me.

"Concisely," Ember said.

"Right. Charley Eye could pass this class with a grade of a 'B,' even if he doesn't complete this DNA project. However, you, Ember, without placing in one of the top

85

three positions in the science fair, will receive an 'F' in my class, and after conferring with your other teachers, your overall grade is barely a 'C.' If you get an 'F' in science, you will not be promoted to sophomore in the fall."

"What!!??"

"You'll have to repeat your freshman year."

"What about English? I know I've got a good grade in there?"

"Yes, your father said you'll get a 'B,' and maybe an 'A', but English won't save you."

She scowled at Mr. Flanders, then at me.

"*Voya abandoner el proyecto de DNA. No me vas a atrapar de nuevo,*" (I'm going to drop out of the DNA project. I'm not going to let you trap me again) I said.

Her mouth fell open. "*Voy a tener que hacer este ano otra vez!*" (I'll have to do this year over again!)

I shrugged. "*Realmente no me importa una mierda.*" (I really don't give a shit.)

"What are you two talking about?"

"He wants to drop out of the project," Ember said. "Can we trade partners with one of the other teams?"

"I checked with them. Crammer is the only one who'd partner with you, but none of them would take Charley Eye on. So the teams are set, and unless someone dies, they won't be changed."

I glanced at Ember, trying not to smile. "*Demasiado. Te das cuenta de que cuando soy un senior, seras un junior, si no fallas otro ano,*"(Too bad. You do realize when I'm a senior you'll be a junior, if you don't fail another year).

She folded her arms and blew a puff of air from her nose.

Ember's Spanish was pretty good. She spoke and understood the language perfectly. Her problem was in writing.

The greatest difficulties in learning Spanish are gender, number, and grammar agreement, verb forms and moods, as well as understanding what makes words feminine or masculine.

She could carry on a great conversation in Spanish but failed most of her written exams, and consequently, she was failing the Spanish class.

I'd learned Spanish, as well as Portuguese, from Catalina. She was a wonderful instructor in languages, music, and love.

I stared at Ember and folded my arms.

"Well?" Mr. Flanders said.

She glared at me. "*Que tengo que hacer para que te quedes conmigo en el proyecto?*" (What do I have to do for you to stay with me on the project?).

"*Admite lo que me hiciste.* (Admit what you did to me.)

"*Jodete.*" (Fuck you). She stood and stormed out of the room.

"What did she say?" Mr. Flanders asked.

"Um...I think she said, 'Forget it.'"

* * * * *

On Friday night, after supper, we sat with Mom and Dad at the cleared dinner table as they talked about what to do with $72.50 we'd earned that week. Most of it came from selling walnuts and firewood.

This was a lot of money, and the $2.65 electric bill was already paid.

"The walnut season will be over in about three weeks," Dad said.

"We have to be careful how we spend this money. It

87

might get us through the winter if you can sell more firewood."

"Me and the boys can cut a lot of firewood," Dad said, "but if that clutch goes out on the truck, we'll be out of business."

"How much for a clutch?" Mom asked.

"I can get a used one for two dollars. A new one will cost twice that much."

"Can you install it?"

"Sure, me and Leo can do that."

"Probably we should get a new one," Mom said. "Then you won't have to worry about it for a while."

"Yeah, a new one will last for years."

"So, that will leave us some money to spare," Mom said, "even after we buy groceries and feed for the livestock." She glanced at me. "What can we do with the extra money to make more money?"

"Charley Eye," Dad said.

I looked at him, then at the tiny smile on Mom's face.

*She's very clever at this little game.*

"You ready to play tomorrow night?" he asked.

"I'm ready, but will anyone show up to listen to a criminal's music?"

"Knowing these hillbillies, probably more people will come to your shows."

"Maybe, but I can't keep borrowing Mr. Landers's guitar."

"What if you had a small one of your own?"

*All right, Dad. You're on the right track. But a small guitar would sound like a ukulele. That won't do.*

"I could maybe play a little one, but it might not sound very good."

"You think we could get a used guitar?" Mom asked

Dad. "A regular-sized one. Then, if it doesn't work for Charley Eye, we'll sell it to get our money back."

"Hmm..." Dad stared at me.

"Why does he get a guitar and I don't?" D.L. whined.

"Can you play a guitar?" Dad asked him.

"Better than that twerp, I bet."

"All right," Dad said. "We'll see. Mom, on Monday afternoon you and me will take a load of walnuts to Springfield, then we'll hit some second-hand stores to see what we can find."

"I think that's a great idea," Mom said.

I smiled and nodded.

"Then we'll see which of our boys can play the thing," Dad said.

I glanced around at my brothers.

*I'm pretty sure I know who that'll be.*

* * * * *

After school on Monday, while Mom and Dad were in Springfield, I asked James to help me make something.

"What?" he asked.

"I need a slice of a log the size of a dinner plate, and about an inch thick."

"What for?"

"If you'll help me cut it, I'll show you."

"All right. Let's go get the crosscut saw."

With me on one end of the saw and James on the other, we cut into a pine log. I was already taller than James, and a bit stronger, so it didn't take long to saw through the twelve-inch log.

"It can't have any knots," I said, "or else it'll split."

He picked up the piece we'd just cut. "We better cut

another one."

After two more tries, we had a nice, solid one.

"Now I need some tools."

In the barn, I found a hammer, chisel, and rasp. I used the rasp to shape the top of the circle of wood into a dome shape, then chiseled out the bottom into a bowl shape. After removing the bark, I shaped the edges into smooth curves.

"You making a wooden plate?" James asked.

"Sort of, but it's not for eating."

I chiseled out more chips of wood, then used sandpaper to smooth all the surfaces. When I finished, it was thin and lightweight.

"Let's try it," I said.

Out in the barnyard, I held it edgewise to my chest, then flicked it out away from me. It flew over thirty yards.

"Wow." James ran to get it. He threw it back toward me, but it hit the ground five feet in front of him.

"Turn it over the other way," I said.

He did, and it flew toward me, curving a bit to the left. As it floated down, I ran to catch it.

"Good one," I yelled.

James ran back to me, took the disk, and looked it over. "What makes it fly like that?"

"It's the shape, sort of like an airplane wing." *No, too much information. How could I know that?* "I guess."

He threw it toward the house, and it flew almost to the back porch.

"What do you call that thing?" James asked. "A flying plate?"

"Yeah, or we could call it a Frisbee."

"Frisbee, huh? I like it. Let's show it to the other guys."

*This should be fun. I wonder what I could use to*

*make a hula hoop and Rubik's Cube?*

All five of us were in the front yard, tossing the Frisbee, when Mom and Dad pulled into the driveway. It was almost dark.

"Charley Eye, look what we've got," Mom said as she stepped down from the truck with a cardboard box.

Dad got out of the driver's side with a guitar case.

"Looks like a piano, Mom," I said.

Dad laughed. It had been a long time since he had anything to laugh about.

"We found a used guitar," Mom said, "for eight dollars."

"That's a pretty good deal," I said. "What's in the box?"

"Some papers. Let's go inside and take a look."

Dad opened the guitar case on the kitchen table. He took out the guitar and handed it to D.L. "Okay, son. Let's see what you can do."

"Oh, boy," D.L. said. "I bet I can play it."

He strummed the strings, making some noise, but not quite musical. "I think it's busted." He handed it to James.

James strummed it and started singing *When She Comes 'Round The Mountain*. He sang pretty well, but the notes weren't actually music.

He offered it to Vern Jr., and his playing was about the same as D.L.'s.

While he played, I opened the box. "Sheet music!"

"Yeah," Mom said. "They gave us the whole boxful with the guitar."

"This is great."

I leafed through the pages. *Wow, this is exactly what I need.* I smiled when I found a particular sheet and laid it out on the table.

"See what Charley Eye can do with it," Wayne said.

I took the instrument from Vern Jr., strummed the strings, then adjusted the A and D strings. I tried it again and adjusted once more.

I played the first few notes of *You're Nobody Till Somebody Loves You*. Then I pulled the sheet of music I'd found in the box over in front of me. When I played the first twelve notes, everyone laughed. I started over, and James sang along.

"She'll be coming 'round the mountain when she comes..."

The others joined him as I played.

Mom stood beside me to read the words from the sheet. "She'll be driving six white horses when she comes."

Dad joined her on the next verse. "Oh, we'll all go out to meet here when she comes."

At the end, everyone clapped, except D.L.

"Where did you learn to read music?" Dad asked.

"In school.  Mr. Landry gave us a lesson on it last week."

"How about this one?" Mom showed me a sheet she'd picked out.

"Maybe I can."

I read through the music. *Yeah, that's pretty easy.*

"Okay, I'll try to play it, and you sing. Let me play a little, then I'll start over."

I played the first ten notes. "Okay, I think I've got it."

Mom sang *You Are My Sunshine* as I played. On the second verse, Dad slipped his arm around her and joined in the song.

At the end, I clapped my hands. "You and Dad sound really good together."

"Well, I don't sound so good." Mom took Dad's

hand. "But your dad has a great voice."

"You are such a liar." He kissed her on the cheek.

"Hey," James said. "Look at this." He pulled a sheet from the stack.

"What is it?" Wayne asked.

"*This Land is Your Land*," James said. "Can you play it?"

"Let me read it." I hummed the notes as I read the words to myself. "Okay, here we go."

Everyone knew the words, and it was easy to play.

*Good, my fingertips are finally beginning to toughen up.*

The old guitar looked like it'd had a rough life, but it sounded good. That box of sheet music was more valuable than the guitar. I knew quite a few of the songs, and after a couple weeks of playing from the sheet music, it wouldn't seem too unreasonable for me to start writing my own—well, that is, copying a few hits from the iPad.

After a week, I'd 'written' ten songs. I felt bad about stealing other people's work, but in actuality, in 1945, most of them hadn't even been born.

*So, was it really stealing? Probably. But who was to sue me? Unborn singers? Unconceived lawyers?*

By taking ideas from the future and setting them free in the past, I was fundamentally changing the history of mankind. What would become of my actions? I had no idea. My only consolation was that without my intervention in the events of the late 1940s, global warming would destroy humanity by 2100. Could anything I might do be worse than that?

* * * * *

I began taking my guitar to the bleachers to practice. No

one at school wanted to hear me play, even the new songs. Since I was an accused sex offender and probably destined for jail, none of the students wanted to be seen with me. I couldn't blame them because I probably wouldn't hang around with a criminal either.

After I finished my sandwich and played *Tonight You Belong To Me*, I looked across the football field at the seats where Patsy, Melody, and I used to sit. Now the two of them had new friends and ate with them in the cafeteria.

I saw them earlier that morning, in the hall, walking with two boys. They were laughing at something Patsy had said and Melody held hands with her new boyfriend; Henry Witt.

* * * * *

When science class was over, Ember stopped me at the door.

"All right," she said.

I pushed past her and turned toward history class.

"Will you just wait a minute?"

"Will you just get the hell away from me?"

She grabbed my arm. "I'll do what you want."

I jerked my arm from her. "You'll do what?"

"I'll admit that I tricked you," she whispered.

"Admit to whom?"

"Whoever you want. I am *not* going to repeat my freshman year."

"All right. In the cafeteria, in front of everybody."

Ember stared at me. "You son-of-a-bitch."

"Yes, I am."

She watched the kids walking by, giving us the eye.

"Okay. When?"

I couldn't believe she was agreeing to do this.

94

"Today, music class, in the cafeteria."

"I'll be there." She turned and marched away.

I watched her go to Crammer and loop her arm in his.

*Why do I feel like a dog being tricked into chasing a stick again?*

* * * * *

At three that afternoon, I took my guitar to the cafeteria, stepped onto the makeshift stage, and turned on the mic.

As soon as I took the stage, half the students left the room. When I started playing, more of them filed out.

Ember came in at a quarter past three. She came up on stage, put her hand over the mic, and glanced around at the twelve students who remained.

"All right," she said. "This isn't so bad. Just a few kids."

"Yeah. You ready?" I asked.

She took her hand from the mic and nodded.

When she cleared her throat and took a deep breath, I stepped back, knelt, and plugged the microphone jack into the school's PA system.

"I have to tell you people something," she said into the mic.

The two loudspeakers behind us probably drowned out the sound of her voice echoing down the hallways and into all the classrooms and offices.

"Charley Eye didn't attack me in the science classroom."

The kids in the room stared at her, and me.

Ember looked at me. "Is that enough?" she whispered.

I shook my head and rolled my hand for her to go

on.

She cleared her throat again. "I tore my blouse open and acted as if he did it."

The door eased open. Patsy, Dolly, and Melody came in, followed by three other students, and Mr. Flanders. Ember swallowed. She looked at me but spoke into the mic.

"But I'm not going down by myself."

More kids pushed into the room and stood along the wall.

"Justin Crammer made me do it."

I heard some students gasp, then some murmuring.

Ember's father pushed through the door and marched to the stage. He grabbed her arm to pull her away for the mic.

"What have you done?"

They weren't as far away from the mic as Mr. Coldstream thought; it picked up their voices for everyone to hear.

"It was all a lie, Dad. Justin worked the whole thing out. At exactly two-thirty, I was to get Charley Eye into position, then rip my clothes. Justin said he'd be sure Mr. Flanders and some others would come through the door at two-thirty."

"Good Lord!" Mr. Coldstream looked around at the room, which was by now half-full. "We've got to get out of here. Then I'm going to deal with Crammer."

As they brushed by me, Mr. Coldstream said, "I'm sorry, Charley Eye. I'll talk to you later."

"Thank you, sir." That lifted some of the weight from my shoulders.

After they were out the door, I went to the mic, took a deep breath and said, "Um, I—"

The principal's voice boomed over the PA system.

"Ember Coldstream and Justin Crammer, in my office, now. And Mr. Coldstream, too."

I waited for the students' chatter to die down.

"Well, I-I guess—"

I was interrupted by applause and cheering.

Melody, Dolly, and Patsy came up on stage to hug me, all of them at once.

"I'm sorry," Dolly said, "that we believed all that crap."

"It's okay. I was an idiot for getting sucked into it."

"Yes," Patsy said, "you are an idiot."

We laughed.

"Are we going to play music or what?" Dolly said.

"Let's do it," I said.

Before the day was over, Judge Hamilton dropped the charges against me.

* * * * *

The next Saturday, I asked Dad to take me to the Springfield City Library. He dropped me off, then went to talk to the lawyer to get my new songs copyrighted.

I browsed through the science section of the library. It was amazing to see what was thought to be cutting-edge science in 1946.

Percy Spencer accidentally discovered microwaves could heat food.

Five thousand homes had TV sets, receiving three black and white channels if they were within ten miles of a transmitter.

The first general purpose computer, the ENIAC, was completed. It covered over two thousand square feet of floor space but couldn't do a fraction of what can be done today on a smart watch.

As I was leaving the library, I saw two cardboard boxes full of magazines. On the side of the boxes was written 'FREE'. I reached for one of the magazines.

"*Popular Science*," I whispered.

I took both boxes and started reading as I sat on the sidewalk, waiting for Dad to pick me up.

* * * * *

The school's Science Fair was being presented in the school gym. As Ember and I set up our project, I coached her on answering questions about DNA.

"I'm sick of deoxyribonucleic acid, chromosomes, self-replicating material, and all this other crap," she said, waving a hand toward the three sections of the backdrop where she'd written all the information.

"Yeah," I said, "I know. But just think about how sick you'll be this time next year, sitting in ninth grade science again."

"I am *not* going to do that."

"Okay, then let's ace this presentation, win a medal, and graduate to tenth grade."

"All right. But if I choke, you've got to bail me out."

"I'll be right here with you."

The two boxes of *Popular Science* magazines, along with a half-dozen technical books, were spread out on the table, making us look as nerdy as possible.

The main question asked was always, "What's DNA?"

Amber had memorized everything she'd written on the backdrop. With the rotating double helix and all its colorful components lighted from both sides, it made a pretty impressive display.

Next to our table was the fingerprint analysis

project done by Ryan Foster and Wanda Hoffman. To their left was a large clay model of a Neanderthal guy pulling his smiling bride by the hair. That was Patsy McCarthy's and Justin Crammer's project.

The caveman actually got a lot more attention than we did, and by the end of the day, it was awarded first place.

The fingerprint analysis got second place, and I was happy when Ember and I placed third.

She was ecstatic, and when she looked like she might hug me, I handed her the medal.

"Hang that on your wall of honor," I said.

"I think I will. Thank you, Charley Eye."

"You're welcome. I'm going to congratulate Patsy on her project."

I didn't mention Crammer, who I expect didn't contribute much. As I walked away, I heaved a sigh of relief, glad to be untangled from Ember.

I noticed the Neanderthal woman grinned as her man pulled her toward his cave.

"So," I said from behind Patsy, "why is she smiling?"

She laughed and turned toward me. "Glad to have a date."

Melody was there, and she laughed, too.

I hugged Patsy. "Congratulations on first place."

"And you for third."

"I'm happy with that." When I let her go, Melody hugged me. "You and Ember, huh?"

"Thank God I'll never have to speak to that girl again."

"Do I get a hug, too?"

It was Dolly.

"Oh, yes. I'm getting it from all the pretty girls

today."

I held her longer than I should have. Over her shoulder, I saw Patsy and Melody, grinning.

They began mouthing the words, "Charley and Dolly, sitting in a tree, K-I-S-S-I-N-G..."

"Um...okay." I let go of Dolly, then took her hand. "Let's go practice."

"Practice?" She gave me a mischievous smile.

"Music," I said as we walked away. "But we could go to the malt shop after school."

"Yeah, I'd like that. But I have to be home before six."

"Okay, I'll figure that out."

*I think I've just changed history, or the future. Dolly isn't going to die, and I'll never meet Catalina.*

*I really need a car.*

* * * * *

By the end of March, Dillon Schoolhouse had become a theater every Saturday night. Mrs. Caldwell didn't mind Dad charging a quarter for admission, since we were helping pay the electric bill.

I had over a hundred songs in my repertoire. Many of them came from the box of sheet music, but also several from the 1960s. All but a few were slow songs, because I didn't think those mountain people, mostly Southern Baptists, were ready for rock 'n roll.

We had a pretty good cash flow. Mom took control of the money, because she knew Dad would blow it on that fancy gold watch he always wanted, or he and Leo might go out drinking and burn through five or ten dollars in one night.

I got my first pair of new overalls and asked Mom to cut off the bib and add belt loops to them.

"Can you make the legs into bellbottoms, like the sailor suits?"

"I think so."

I also had her lower the waistline by three inches so the belt went around my upper hips.

She also got me a store-bought blue shirt, which went well with my bellbottom pants.

* * * * *

Two weeks after the science fair, Melody, Dolly, and I waited for Patsy in the hall, near the cafeteria.

Dolly slipped her hand into mine. I smiled and squeezed her hand.

"Do you think Patsy's lost weight?" Melody asked.

"You know what? I was wondering that same thing," I said. "I thought she looked a little slimmer, but I'm not sure."

Finally, we saw her coming toward us.

I leaned close to Melody. "Yes, definitely."

"And she smiles more. Look at her, she's really happy."

"Hi," Patsy said. "Been waiting long?"

"No, not long." I grinned.

Melody and Dolly smiled, too.

"Why are you people so happy?"

"You've lost weight," Melody said.

"You can tell?"

"Yep," I said. "We noticed. How much have you lost?"

"Twelve pounds."

"That's wonderful," I said.

Melody hugged her. "I am so proud of you."

"Did you remember?" Patsy asked. "I'm buying lunch today."

"You better be," I said. "We didn't bring our sandwiches."

Inside, we picked up trays and started down the serving line.

"This is a first for me." I picked up a small bowl of mashed potatoes.

"Me, too." Melody took some coleslaw. "This is so exciting."

Dolly reached for a salad.

Patsy took a plate with a chicken fried steak. "I'm starving."

Crammer sat at a table with his pals. I noticed him say something to his buddies as they watched us. His pals laughed.

"Hold my place." I went toward their table. "You got something to say, Crammer?" I leaned on the table, very close to his face.

"What if I do?"

"Say it," I said. "If I don't like it, I *will* cram it down your throat, along with my fist."

"I just said it must be nice to have three girlfriends."

"And you think that's funny?"

He glanced at his pals. They looked at me.

I stared them down.

Crammer kept quiet.

"That's what I thought. If I see anything at this table..." I gave each one of them a hard look, "...that I don't like, I'll settle up with each one of you after school."

I waited for a reply. None came.

Back in line, I spoke to Patsy. "Hey, you got me

some black-eyed peas."

"Yeah. You like those, right?"

"That, I do."

Our four meals, plus milk for each of us, cost Patsy $2.92.

We found an empty table. Dolly and I sat on one side, and they on the other.

"Tomorrow, I'm buying," I said as I opened my milk carton.

"And I'll get the next day," Melody said.

"And I buy the next day," Dolly said.

I cut into my pork chop and looked around as I chewed. "So, this is what it's like, eating like regular people."

Patsy giggled. "Yeah, I like it."

"So much better than the bleachers." Melody sipped her milk.

"You have any new songs?" Dolly asked.

I wiped my lips on a napkin. "Yes. I've written two new songs." I took some folded papers from my hip pocket. "This one, I call *Unchained Melody*." I unfolded the three pages of paper and passed one to each of the girls.

"Aw," Patsy said. "You wrote a song for Melody." She grinned at her friend and read the lyrics.

I took a bite of mashed potatoes. "Maybe."

"I love the words," Dolly said.

"Are you..." Melody sniffed and put down her fork. She took a napkin to wipe her cheek. "Have you..." She kept her face down, letting her hair fall to hide her eyes. "Have you written one named *Dolly*?"

"Not yet." I took a bite as Patsy looked up from the music. "But I'm working on *Patricia*."

That brought a smile to her face. She went back to her food as she read the music.

Melody wiped her cheeks again. "Drums in this one?"

"Oh, yes." I looked at Patsy's tray. "That's the most I've ever seen you eat."

"Yeah, I know. Everything tastes so good."

"Is there some reason for this change in your appetite?"

"Mom took me to the doctor three weeks ago, and he said I have a condition called hypothyroidism."

"Really?" I smiled.

"I'm getting a shot once a week, and he told me to eat normally, like everyone else."

"That's great news," Melody said.

"Mom's been taking my clothes in so they won't look baggy. She said if I keep this up, I can get all new outfits next month."

I held out my fist for a bump, and the other girls did the same.

"What did you say to Crammer a while ago?" Patsy asked.

"I...um...just asked if he and his lapdogs wanted to eat with us."

Melody giggled. "What did he say?"

I grinned. "He said they would love to but they had a previous engagement."

They laughed, and that made me laugh.

I drank some milk and glanced at Dolly. "Would it be hard to learn to play the saxophone?"

She swallowed a bite of smashed potatoes. "Hard for you, but not for me."

"Dang it," I said.

"You've got a dynamite drummer," Patsy said, "why do you want a sax?"

"Just to add a little depth." I glanced at Dolly. "But

if you don't think you can do it..."

Dolly punched me in the shoulder. "I'll ask Mr. Landers if he has a saxophone hiding in his closet."

* * * * *

We began to see strangers show up on Saturday nights. I watched the newcomers closely as I played my music.

I had to be sure some slick music producer didn't rope Dad into a rotten contract. I had a birthday coming up in December, but a teenage kid giving legal advice to his 38-year-old father probably wouldn't fly. It would have to be Mom to keep us out of trouble.

On a Saturday night in November, the schoolhouse was packed. Dad was still charging just a quarter at the door, but with more than a hundred people, that would give us a pretty good night.

About twenty minutes into the show, I saw Dad talking to a tall guy in a shiny suit. He wore a string tie and fancy Stetson hat.

*Maybe that's the guy I've been waiting for.*

After two more songs, I took a break and went to sit beside Mom. "We have to have a serious—"

Two girls came to stand before me. They were maybe eleven or twelve years old.

"Can we...um...h-have your autograph?" the curly blonde asked.

This was something new.

*How cool, autographs.*

"Sure, but I don't have anything to write on."

Each of them held out little notebooks, like diaries. And they had colored pencils—one with red lead, the other blue.

"What's your name?" I asked the blonde.

105

"Alice."

"'Alice,'" I wrote, "'thank you for coming to my show.'"

After my signature I added a smiley face and handed it back to Alice.

The other girl's name was Veronica.

"'Hi, Veronica. The next song's for you.'" I wrote in her diary.

Her face flushed as she stared at the floor. She then leaned down and kissed my cheek so fast, I didn't even see it coming.

The two girls hurried away, giggling and whispering.

"That was sweet, Charley Eye," Mom said.

"I never expected that."

"I think you're becoming famous."

"Maybe, but listen. Take a look at that guy talking to Dad."

She glanced at him. "Looks like a city slicker."

"That's exactly what he is. And I think he might be from a music company."

"Really?" She turned to look at him again.

"He might be. If he offers Dad a contract, be sure he doesn't sign anything until you get a chance to look at it. And if it's a long contract, you better get a lawyer to read it."

"How do you know all this stuff?"

*Yeah, that was a mouthful for a fifteen-year-old.*

"I've read almost every book in the school library. That's only about 500 books, but you know I have a good memory, so I've learned a lot over the past six months."

"I'll say you have."

"One thing I remember is that city slickers will take advantage of country people who might not know much about handling money. He could easily trick Dad into something where a fast-talking shyster could make a lot of money and we'd get little or nothing."

"How old are you, really?"

"Seventy-nine." I grinned at her.

"And I thought you were fifteen." She smiled back at me. "Okay, I see what you're talking about, but why would he even offer us a contract?"

"Because he thinks he could sell some of my songs on records."

"Ah, I see."

"When I go back on stage, you need to pull Dad aside and be sure he doesn't sign anything."

"Okay, but you know lawyers cost a lot of money."

"Yes, but have you seen how the crowds have grown over the past three months?"

She glanced around at the packed room. "Yeah. You go sing, and I'll talk to Dad."

I was surprised when I stepped onto the stage; the audience applauded before I even picked up my guitar.

I watched Mom walk toward the back, then I looked around until my eyes fell on Veronica. She smiled and waved.

After I strummed a couple chords, I winked at her and sang *Stand By Me.*

As I sang, I saw the city slicker hand some papers and a fountain pen to Dad. Mom reached for the papers, then handed the pen back to the guy. She began reading as the guy scowled at her.

*Good job, Mom.*

I sang *American Pie,* followed by *Ring of Fire.* In the middle of *Ring of Fire,* I added a little moonwalk.

*Thank you, Michael Jackson.*

Dad wasn't happy when we got home.

"You don't think I'm capable of handling a contract?"

"Yes," Mom said. "I think you're quite capable."

"Then why did you stop me from signing it?"

"Did you read it?"

"I read 'Five hundred dollars up front.' That's all I need to know."

"Did you read the last paragraph on the second page?" she asked.

"I glanced through it. Legal gobbledygook. Nobody reads that junk."

"I agree."

"Then what's the problem? Do you know what we could do with five hundred dollars?"

"We could buy a secondhand car," Mom said. "Get some decent clothes for the boys, go to a café for a nice dinner...lots of things."

"Well, then we should sign Mr. Ditcher's contract."

"Listen to this." Mom flipped to the second page of the contract. "Promisor agrees to assign benefits of all present and future intellectual development of aforementioned minor to Promisee, and further agrees to negate any anticipatory repudiation, and hereby forgoes any and all monetary benefits beyond amount declared in paragraph 1-3 above and notwithstanding within and under the provisions of all legal statutes, and Promisor agrees not to enter into any contracts with competitors of Promisee, and Promisor hereby acquits, exonerates, and forever discharges from and against Promisee any legal proceedings, thus the parties to this agreement do mutually covenant and agree to any and all provisions herein contained.”

“Pure mumbojumbo,” Dad said.

It means, I wanted to tell him, we’d sell every song I might produce for the rest of my life, for five hundred dollars. We’d never get another cent, we could never sign with another record producer, and we’d give up rights to sue Ditcher in court.

“It means, I think,” Mom said, “we’d get five hundred, but nothing more, even though Charley Eye might write a hundred new songs. He would be working for Draven Ditcher for nothing for the rest of his life.”

“That’s what it says?” Dad asked.

“I think so. We really need to get a lawyer to look at this.”

“Do you know how much a lawyer costs? I heard they charge five dollars an hour, just to explain what’s written on a piece of paper.”

“Dad,” I said, “can I ask a question?”

“What is it, son?”

“How much did we make tonight?”

He took a paper bag from the old navy p-coat he’d draped over the back of his chair. He dumped the money out on the table, then he and Mom counted it.

“Thirty-seven-fifty,” Mom said.

“How many Saturday nights would it take to make 500 dollars?”

“Hmm...” Dad said. “Anyone have a pencil and paper?”

*Thirteen weeks, come on.*

Vern Jr. got his Big Chief tablet and pencil, then slid it across the table to Mom.

She did the math. “About three months.”

“And,” I said, “no tricky contracts.”

Dad stared at me for a long time. “I wonder if we

could rent the Fordland High School gym."

*Yes, that place holds five hundred people! Perfect.*

* * * * *

On December 1st, my birthday, I wrote a new song, *Jingle Bell Rock*. The next Saturday night, I added it to my routine. It became very popular, just as it did in 1957 when Bobby Helms sang it for the first time.

* * * * *

In January, Dad went to the *Springfield Leader* newspaper office and paid six dollars for a hundred fliers advertising my next show to be held in the Fordland High School gym. He and Mom posted the fliers all around Springfield, Fordland, and Seymour.

* * * * *

I stood on the stage, petrified.

*So many people. Come on, you've done this a million times. San Francisco, Munich, Saigon...this is only a few hundred people. Just do it!*

The gym bleachers were packed, and thirty or forty people were standing in the back.

Some of the audience began to squirm and whisper as they watched me. I glanced at Mom. She smiled.

I took a deep breath, swallowed, and strummed the guitar. After a few notes, I was into it and back to my old troubadour self.

My first song was *The Lion Sleeps Tonight*. Slow and easy, not many words. By the third chorus, several people were singing along with me.

*Puff The Magic* Dragon came next, followed by *Scarborough Fair.* And then *Take Me Home, Country Roads.*

*All right, I think these teens are ready for something faster.*

I did *Girls Just Want to Have Fun*, followed by *Jonny B. Goode.* That got some of the girls on their feet.

The voice of a teenage boy doesn't normally have much inflection or depth. But I used my voice training to give it some character.

My voice teacher was a Brazilian brunette.

She, and the disaster that set me on a course of personal destruction, took place in my other life, the one already played out, and the one I was now reconstructing.

How I got to Rio at the age of seventeen began with the double tragedy that hit the Riot Legion gang in our senior year of high school. We weren't a street gang; just a handful of pals who'd been together since ninth grade. There was George Crocker, Merle Edmonson, Gloria Jason, Wanda McCracken, Dolly Anna Dubois, and me. We picked the name 'Riot Legion' to make us sounded bad-ass. If it ever came to a confrontation with a real street gang, we'd probably compete with each other in a foot race to escape.

Merle had left high school when he was a sophomore, to work construction. The foreman on a building project sent him to the bottom of a twelve-foot-deep ditch to repair on a water line. Heavy rains the night before had left eighteen inches of mud and water in the bottom of the ditch, and in addition, the rain had weakened the sandy soil on both sides.

As Merle was bailing water from the bottom of the ditch, the sides of the ditch gave way and caved in, burying our pal under tons of dirt and rocks. The other workers tried to dig him out, but they didn't get to him in time.

The Riot Legion was devastated by the loss of our friend, but more tragedy was on the way.

All of us, the three boys and three girls, always said we were just best friends, nothing more. Anyway, that's what we said out loud.

Two days after Merle's funeral, Dolly Dubois committed suicide. She left a note saying she couldn't go on without the love of her life; Merle. Her mother found her in the bathtub with her left wrist slit.

I was wiped out. Dolly had admitted her love for Merle too late, and I'd never been able to work up the courage to tell Dolly I'd been in love with her since the beginning of high school.

The remaining four members of our gang drifted apart, except for me and George. It was the end of childhood for all of us. But for me and George, the deaths of our two close friends coming just days apart thrust us into hopeless despair.

We hit the road, hitchhiking south. We had no idea where we were going, but three days later we woke up in a flophouse in Villa Acuna, Mexico, across the border from Del Rio, Texas.

At sixteen, we had no knowledge of how the world worked. We were broke, hungry, and homesick.

"I'm going back," George said.

"How?"

"Same way we got here."

"Going back to what? School? And all those terrible memories?"

"Yeah, that and my mom's cooking. Aren't you starving?"

"Yes," I said. "But I'm not going back."

We split up that day, and I never saw George again.

I found a job picking cotton. It didn't take any skill

or knowledge of the Spanish language; just a strong back and weak mind.

Working my way south, I held a job just long enough to earn a few pesos to get me farther away from Dolly's grave.

How far south could I go? To the tip of South America? Then what? I really didn't care.

After two months on the road, my scraggly beard was two inches long, my unkempt hair was a mess, and my one set of clothes were wearing out. But still, I worked for a few days, then caught a bus or walked the highways. I used my pocketknife to cut my ragged jeans off at the knees and tied a red bandana around my head to keep my hair back. I didn't know what I looked like, but I was pretty much a homeless bum.

I turned seventeen on a banana plantation in Guatemala. More mindless labor, but at least I was building up some muscle.

It was July, the middle of winter, when I stepped down from a bus in Rio de Janeiro, Brazil. I carried an old backpack I'd found in a trash heap in Honduras. I had eighty-seven pesos, which amounted to about nine dollars, and my pocketknife.

I slumped into a seat in the bus station, almost done for. My only plans were to find some manual labor to make at least enough money to buy a coat. I'd become accustomed to one meal a day, which was usually a burrito and water, so I ignored my empty stomach.

An hour or so passed. I sat with my head back, staring at the vaulted ceiling, my mind halfway between oblivion and sleep. Suddenly, I heard music; beautiful music.

I sat up, glancing around.

*Guitar. Where?*

Over in the corner, leaning back against a marble pillar, was a girl, a dark-eyed teen, strumming an ancient guitar.

I didn't recognize the music, probably because all I knew about music was the rock 'n roll I'd heard on the radio, but this was beautifully intricate and evocative. I was mesmerized, almost hypnotized.

As I watched her, she slid down to sit on the cold floor at the base of the pillar. Her guitar case was open before her. An old man stopped to listen for a moment, then dropped a coin into her case. I couldn't hear her words, but she apparently thanked him for the donation.

Her clothing was much like mine; worn-out and ragged. A dirty rag ran across her forehead and was tied at the back of her head. If not for my beard, we looked a lot alike.

I went over and sat cross-legged before her.

She glanced at me, then scanned me from head to toe. She grinned.

A woman in high heels and a fur coat walked by, dropping a few coins into the case. Her heels clicked across the tile floor, fading away.

I leaned back to get my hand into my pocket. Pulling out my money; three two-peso bills and a handful of coins, I dropped all of it into her case.

Her eyes widened at the sight of so much money. She looked at me, back at the money, then at me again, wrinkling her brow as she continued to play her beautiful music.

I shrugged. "It's not much."

"*Obrigado.*" She had a beautiful smile.

I'd picked up a few words of Spanish on the road, but this was Portuguese, not too much different than Spanish.

*"De nada."*

She dumped the money from her case and put away the guitar. With the money in her pocket and the strap of the case over her shoulder, she held out her hand to me.

I took her hand to pull myself up from the floor.

*"Tienes hambre?"* (Are you hungry?) she asked in Spanish.

*"Un poco."* (A little)

On the street, we found a pushcart with a variety of hot food. She bought two tacos and a cup of coffee.

We sat on the grass in front of the courthouse. She handed me one of the tacos, and we shared the coffee.

I chewed a bite. *"Donde duermes?"* (Where do you sleep?) "Did I say that right? My Spanish stinks."

"Where do I sleep?" she said in English.

I nodded.

"Wherever."

"Me, too."

She passed me the coffee.

We were quiet, just watching the people walk by in their warm coats and gloves.

She finished her food, then reached for the coffee. "You gave me a lot of money."

I blew a puff of air from my nose. "Right, probably enough for two more tacos."

I wanted to know how she'd ended up on the street, but I doubted she wanted to talk about it, and I certainly didn't want to tell her about my recent ugly past.

She took the empty taco wrapper from me, wadded it up with hers, and stuffed them into the cup. She then stood and swung her guitar over her shoulder.

"Come on," she said.

*"Dlonde?"* I took the trash from her and walked toward a bin on the sidewalk.

*"Para comprarte unos pantalones y medias."* (To buy you some pants and socks.)

At a second-hand store, we found some old jeans and a pair of mismatched wool socks.

"I'm Catalina."

"Charley."

In my warm clothing, we walked to the downtown section, and she took up a spot near the exit from a tall office building.

"You from New York City?"

I laughed. "No. I came from Fordland, Missouri."

"Ah, Cherokee."

"Maybe."

She earned a few coins from the wealthy stockbrokers.

When she started playing and singing *Dream Lover*, I began to sing with her.

She stopped. "Shut up. You're scaring everybody away."

*"Lo siento."* (I'm sorry.)

She went back to the song.

*What a beautiful voice.*

"I wish I had some drums."

After the office building had emptied, she bought six burritos and took me to a railroad overpass on the edge of downtown. Under the bridge, she greeted three people beside a blazing fire; two men and a woman.

*"Este e Charley."* She handed them three of the burritos.

*"Buena noches,"* I said, and they returned my greeting.

In the shadows of the upper beams of the bridge, Catalina unrolled her bedding and shared her blanket with me.

We were up at sunrise, walking toward the bus station.

I told her I'd catch up with her at the office building downtown.

She kissed me and laid out her guitar case.

A seventeen-year-old with a strong back can always get a job, as long as there's no thinking involved.

I found work on the Rio docks, loading sides of beef bound for Europe.

Ten days later, Catalina rented a tiny room for us.

At the end of August, we hired onto a cruise ship on its way to Rotterdam.

She played and sang every night in the dining room, while I backed her up on the drums and sometimes joined her in a duet.

We traveled all over Western Europe, playing every roadhouse, cantina, and beer garden along the way.

She told me singers aren't born; they're trained. She taught me the basics of warming up my vocal cords and breathing properly.

"Drink plenty of water to keep your vocal cords moist. Don't sing from your mouth, but from your diaphragm. And stand up straight."

She gave me scales of notes to push the pitch of my voice to the limits, but probably the most important technique she taught me was how to use vibrato in my voice. This is a regular, pulsating change of pitch, she explained. It's used to add expression to a singer's vocal range. This, she said, will transform your singing. And it did. Soon, I was singing on stage almost as much as she was.

We made pretty good money, but even with our tip jar filling up every night, we had to move on. She and I were alike in our need to see what lay beyond the next horizon.

We talked about everything; our past lives, music, the places we wanted to see. We spoke easily in English, Portuguese, and Spanish, sometimes all three mixed together.

In the middle of October, we arrived in Madrid, where she met a bullfighter. His name was Poco. He was broad-shouldered and wore a tight leotard covering his narrow butt.

Dolly had broken my heart when she killed herself. Catalina had mended it, then crushed it all over again with four words.

"See you in Rio."

She gave me her guitar and left for Barcelona with Poco.

I was as stunned as the bull that had received the blade of Poco's sword on the previous evening.

After moping around Madrid for a week, I signed on to a freighter at Cartagena, Spain. The ancient steamer was headed for the Suez Canal, then on to Hong Kong with a load of dynamite.

I volunteered for the hardest job on the ship: Shoveling coal in the boiler room. I hoped twelve hours a day of hard sweaty labor would burn away any hint of emotions I had left. If that didn't work out, I might toss a shovelful of embers into the dynamite.

There are several four-letter words in the English language, but 'love' was, for me, the most vile of all.

Halfway across the Indian Ocean, I realized Catalina had left me with a gift: Her music.

One night, after washing away the grime of coal dust, I took her guitar to the mess cabin, where I found twenty-three grim Filipino sailors eating fish stew. I cheered them up with *Puff, the Magic Dragon, Sugar*

*Sugar,* and *California Girls.*

I never returned to Rio, but I carried Catalina's music with me for the rest of my life.

* * * * *

Back in the high school gym, I played the first line of *Y M C A*, then swung my guitar to my back and performed the letters, 'Y', 'M', 'C', 'A' with body movements as I sang.

Some of the teen girls in the bleachers, still standing from the last song, got the movements right away. Five of them ran onto the floor and lined up to do the dance steps. I think they were cheerleaders, because they quickly fell into synchronization. They wore pleated plaid knee-length skirts, tight sweaters over cream-colored blouses, and white bobby socks with saddle shoes.

After *Y M C A*, I did the moonwalk. They watched my feet and soon had it down pat. They did it with me. I then danced the *Gangnam Style* pony move, which they got right away. After dancing *The Hype*, I did a few robot steps, then we did all five moves in sequence, much to the delight of the audience. In the *Shiggy* steps, I formed my fingers into a heart shape and held it over my heart. The girls added the heart move into their dancing.

After the third iteration, I touched my forehead, then my heart as I salaamed to the girls.

I spoke into the mic. "Thank you, ladies. I'm going to take a five-minute break before the second half. Let's hear it for the dancers!"

The girls got a great shout-out as they ran back to their seats in the bleachers.

I went to sit with Mom for a little rest.

"You were wonderful." She hugged me. "When did you write all those new songs?"

119

"Um…in school."

"Everyone loved them."

"Uh-oh."

"What?" she asked.

I nodded toward the five cheerleaders coming toward us.

I stood, unsure of what was going to happen. I watched them, swallowed, and tried to smile. The one on the left, a beautiful redhead, leaned in to hug me.

"That was so much fun."

"T-thank you." *Wow, she smells good.*

"Will you do *Y M C A* again, after the break?" another asked.

"Sure."

"What will you do after that one?"

"Um…I don't know. Do you like a fast beat, or slow?"

"Fast, for sure."

"Can we have your autograph?"

"Yeah."

Each one had a copy of the show flier for me to sign. It looked a little different than the one Dad had printed, but with the same wording.

I asked their names as I wrote a note on each flier, then handed them back. After my signature, I added a smiley face, as before.

"Where did you get these fliers, Wendy?" I signed the next one.

"We have a mimeograph machine in the school office."

"Really? How does that work? There you go, Brandy."

"They have a special typewriter that makes the page to be duplicated. They fit that page into the mimeograph, then crank the handle to print as many copies as you want."

"Cool."

"Cool?"

"Um...neat."

After I signed the fifth one, they compared them, giggling.

I signed 'Charley Eye' and drew a different smiley on each one; one with cat whiskers, one with glasses, one winking, another with a hat.

Before I realized what I was doing, I held out my fist for a bump.

They stared at me and my extended fist. Their confused expressions worried me.

"Some people shake hands," I said, "but on my planet, we do fist bumps."

No one moved.

"Like this."

I took Wendy's hand, made it into a fist, then pressed it against my fist. I spread my fingers in a little explosion. "Boom."

One of the girls laughed and held out her fist to me. I bumped it and exploded my fingers.

"Cool," another said as she held out her fist. She exploded her fingers as I did.

They were all delighted with the new gimmick.

*That'll be all over school by Monday afternoon.*

*So, Wendy, Brandy, Mary, Caroline, and Rose Mary. I'll have to remember those names.*

I started the second half with *Sweet Home Alabama*, followed by *Bimbombey*, then *Y M C A*.

During the next song, I noticed Draven Ditcher in his Stetson hat, standing beside the double doors in the back. Beside him was a young woman. It looked like she was writing on a notepad.

I closed the show with *American Pie*, then announced the next show would be on the following Saturday night.

"Goodnight, everyone." I formed my fingers into the heart shape and held it to my chest. "Thank you for coming." Several people returned my heart salute.

Before I got off the stage, I saw a crowd of girls waiting for an autograph.

As we climbed into the truck that night, I said, "I love you, Mom."

The word 'love' still had a bad taste for me, but I knew Mom would never run off with a bullfighter and leave me with a crushed heart.

Funny how I'm living in the body of my fifteen-year-old self but still have my knowledge and feelings of a lifetime.

*I wonder where Catalina is tonight.*

* * * * *

Mom and I sat at the kitchen table, counting the money from her Bell jar. I'd had twelve Saturday night shows since I started performing.

I added up the number of coins we'd stacked on the table. I loved the feel of the silver dollars. I noticed several old ones that would be worth a small fortune sixty years in the future.

I also saw lots of one-dollar bills, and a few fives.

After adding the amount of paper money plus the coins, I said, "Seven hundred fifty-three dollars and thirty-seven cents."

"Holy smokes!" Mom said. "You've done good, son."

"*We've* done good. I think you need to get this

money into a bank and open a checking account."

She smiled. "We haven't had a checking account since 1929."

"Well, maybe it's about time."

"Hey, Charley Eye!" James shouted from the front room. "They're playing your song on the radio."

Mom and I hurried in from the kitchen.

Sure enough, they were playing *Sweet Home Alabama.*

"What the heck?" I whispered.

"That's not your voice," Mom said.

"No, it's some man singing. And they've added a piano and drums."

Dad and Uncle Leo came in from the front porch. "That's your song," Dad said.

I nodded.

He listened for a moment. "Who's singing?"

"We don't know," Mom said.

"What station is that?" Uncle Leo asked.

"KGBX," Mom said. "In Springfield."

"Let's go," Leo said.

"Where?" Dad asked.

"To see who's singing Charley Eye's song."

"I'm going, too." I ran to follow them out to the truck.

* * * * *

At the radio station, Dad asked to see the manager.

"Yes, how can I help you?"

"You were playing *Sweet Home Alabama* a little while ago," Leo said.

The man glanced from Leo to Vern. "Yes."

"Where did you get it?" Dad asked.

He was a fat man, bald, with a walrus mustache. He wore a colorful wide tie, and his long sleeves were rolled up above his elbows.

"It's on a record."

"A record?" I asked.

He looked at me and nodded.

"Where did the record come from?" Leo asked.

"Why all the questions?"

"My son wrote that song," Dad said.

"Your son?"

"Yes." Dad put his hand on my shoulder.

The man laughed. "He's a kid."

"He's Charley Eye," Leo said.

"Holy cow!"

"Yeah," Dad said.

The man held out his hand to Dad. "I'm Richard Pritchard."

"Vern Brindley."

"Come with me."

He led us into a room where a man sat at a microphone in a soundproof booth, behind a large pane of glass. Another man stood at a turntable outside the booth.

"Eddie," Richard said to the turntable guy, "where's that *Sweet Home Alabama* record?"

Eddie picked up the record and handed it to the manager. It was large, one of the old 78 rpm records.

He read the label. "Draven Ditcher Productions."

"That son-of-a—" Dad glanced at me. "Ditcher. He stole our music."

"Eddie," Richard said, "please tell me you checked the copyright on this record."

"Yes, sir. You know I don't play any new ones unless I verify the copyright first."

"Who holds the copyright?"

"Draven Ditcher Productions."

"Date of the copyright?"

"January twelfth, nineteen forty-six, three months ago."

I remembered seeing Ditcher standing in the back of the gym at one of my performances. That woman next to him must have been writing down the lyrics of the song as I sang.

"Did you copyright the song?" Richard asked Dad. "If you have a copyright prior to January twelfth, you can file charges against this guy."

Dad heaved a sigh and stared at the floor. "No. We didn't copyright it."

"I'm sorry, guys. I've heard Charley Eye perform, and I've no doubt he wrote this song, but as long as Ditcher holds the copyright, he can do anything he wants with it."

"There's nothing we can do?" Leo asked.

Richard shook his head, then looked at me. "But I will tell you this; get all your other songs copyrighted, now, today. You don't want to lose any more."

"How do we do that?" Dad asked.

"Our station has a lawyer who specializes in this kind of stuff. You need to get a copy of each of your songs to him, right away. And let's hope Ditcher hasn't already stolen more of them."

"A lawyer," Dad said. "More expenses."

"Yeah," Leo said. "But if you don't do it, you're going to lose a lot more money than you're going to spend on a lawyer."

"I guess you're right."

I watched Eddie place a record on the turntable, then after a hand motion from the guy at the microphone, he lowered the tone arm to start the record playing. We couldn't hear the music, so he must've been feeding the soundtrack directly into the station's transmitter.

"Mr. Pritchard," I said.

"Yes?"

"Do you ever broadcast live music?"

"No. Our disk jockey," he waved his hand toward the guy at the mic, "talks about the music, then Eddie plays the record when the DJ is ready for it to be broadcast."

"I have some songs I've never performed."

"Really?"

I nodded. "If Dad puts your lawyer to work on the copyright paperwork, would you like for me to sing some of my new music, right here in your studio?"

He stared at me for a moment. "How old are you?"

"Seventy-nine. How old are you?"

He laughed.

Richard asked me to come in on Monday at 5 in the afternoon for a half-hour show.

"We'll try it for a week and see how people respond," he said.

"Okay," Dad said. "We'll be here on Monday."

* * * * *

During the radio show on Monday, the DJ interviewed me on the air, between songs.

"How long have you been singing, Charley Eye?"

"About six months."

"Where did the name 'Charley Eye' come from?"

"My brother, James. Mom named me for my uncle Charles, who was murdered in a revenge killing in nineteen twenty-two."

"What? A revenge killing?"

"Yes. My grandmother shot a woman she caught in a haystack with my grandfather. She shot her six times

126

with an old black powder pistol. She was so close to the other woman, the burning powder set the woman's dress on fire. She was already dead, but my grandmother leaned down to pat the flames out. Then she waited for the sheriff."

"Holy mackerel!"

"Three months later, two women in a Model T Ford ran over my grandmother's son, Charles, as he rode his bike down the side of the highway, on his way to take lunch to my grandfather."

"That's terrible, but how did that get you your name?"

"The story I heard is that James said when I was born and Mom picked the name Charles for me, I'd be the first Charles in our family, so I should be called Charles the First, like the King of England. So he wrote out my name as 'Charley I.'"

"Oh, I get it."

"Later on, the 'I' became 'E-y-e,' and it stuck with me."

"That's a great story. Now, what are you going to sing next?"

* * * * *

The following Saturday morning, someone honked as they drove into our driveway; it was Richard. He got out of his new Packard, with a cardboard box under his arm.

"You people need to get a phone." He reached to shake hands with Dad.

"They haven't strung the telephone wires out this far yet," Dad said.

"This is for you." He gave me the box.

"What is it?" I opened the flaps on the box.

"Letters."

"People are sending fan mail to the station."

"Really?" I tore one open and read to myself. *Wow!* I read it aloud. "Dear Charley Eye. I love the sound of your voice. When is your next live performance? How much are tickets? Where will it be? My daughter wants to meet you. Love and kisses, Jenney."

Mom opened one and laughed. "Dear Charley Eye. Will you marry me? Kerry."

We laughed, too .

I read another one. "I listen to you every day on my radio. I'm crippled and can't get out much. Your music brings me a half-hour of happiness every day. Love you, Linda."

Mom opened one. "Will you perform at our next football home game? Wendy." She followed her name with a smiley kitten face.

"Dad, what do you think?"

"Sure. Can we charge them for it?"

"We could, but I just want to try out some new songs."

"But they won't be copyrighted."

"I don't think old Ditcher will be at a high school football game."

"Yeah, probably not."

"If the kids like the new songs, we'll go see the lawyer to get copyrights on them."

* * * * *


On Monday night, every seat was taken in the high school stadium. Forty or fifty people stood behind the end zones.

The school maintenance men had built a temporary stage they could pull out of the way when the game started.

They also set up a mic and PA system.

I started out with *Kodachrome*, but someone shouted, "We can't hear you."

Wendy ran over to the PA system and adjusted the sound. She got some squelch, then turned the dial back a little.

I began the song again, and soon Wendy smiled and clapped her hands to the beat.

Next I played *I Got You Babe*, then *The Sound of Silence*.

After that song, I held out my hand to Wendy. "Get up here."

As soon as I started playing, she laughed and shouted, "*Y M C A!*"

She began singing, and I remained silent as I played the guitar and we performed the dance steps together. Soon, all the students were on their feet, performing the *Y M C A*.

When we finished the piece, I waved my hand toward her and bowed.

She got a round of applause and whistles from the boys as she jumped down from the stage.

I played *Sugar Shack*, then closed with *Born to be Wild*.

Wendy waited for me to jump down from the stage.

"Can I ask a favor?" I asked her.

"Sure."

"Can you make some copies for me on the school's mimeograph?"

"Copies of what?"

I handed her a sheet of paper with five blank music staffs. "I need those to write music."

"Oh, okay."

"Tell your principal we'll be happy to pay for them."

"I don't think they'll mind if I use the machine during the lunch hour," she said.

"If you can do that, I'll write a song for you."

"Really, for me?"

I nodded.

Written in 1967, *Wendy* was a big hit for *The Association*. It went straight to number one on the *Billboard Hot 100*.

I changed the lyrics a little bit in *Brandy* from 1972. Sang by *The Looking Glass*. In my version, I put Brandy to work serving milkshakes in a malt shop instead of laying whiskey down in a bar.

At the next Saturday concert, I performed *Wendy* and *Brandy*, much to the delight of the two girls.

* * * * *

One evening after school, I asked Dad a question, "Can you take me to a beer joint?"

"What?"

"One with a jukebox."

"Why a jukebox?"

"I want to see what kind of music they play."

"Get your hat, Mom," Dad said. "Looks like we're going out for a beer."

* * * * *

Inside *The Rusty Nail Bar and Café,* it was smoky and loud.

Mom and Dad sat at the bar and ordered Pabst Blue Ribbon longnecks.

A small stage was at the end of the room, beyond the dance floor. On the stage was a set of drums, an upright piano, and two guitars leaning in their stands.

The jukebox began playing *Chattanooga Choo Choo*. It was a colorful Wurlitzer with a glass front, where I could see the mechanism of the record changer.

As I watched, a man came over, inserted a nickel, and pressed a button on the front.

When *Chattanooga Choo Choo* finished, a metal arm came down to grasp the record by the edges. It lifted the record, then placed it in a slot on a circular rack. With a series of clicks and whirls, the rack rotated a few inches. The arm reached to pick up a new record and place it on the turntable.

*Boogie Woogie Bugle Boy* began to play.

*That's a big record for just one song.*

It was a 78 rpm shellac disk, about twelve inches across. And it was fragile, compared to the vinyl of the new 45s coming soon.

I went to sit on a barstool beside Mom. She was laughing at something Dad had said. They were both smoking.

"Bring my boy a RC," Dad said to the bartender.

The bartender set the huge bottle of RC Cola before me.

"Can I sing on your stage?" I asked him as I lifted the bottle for a sip.

He laughed. "You can make all the racket you want for all I care. But you better ask the band leader before you do anything."

"Okay."

Four men filed in from the side of the stage and took up their instruments.

I went to the front of the stage.

"Do you mind if I sing a song?"

The man at the microphone knelt down at the edge

of the stage. "What did you say?" He cupped a hand behind his ear.

I repeated my question.

He stood. "Hey, Mike," he yelled.

The bartender turned toward him and lifted his chin.

The bandleader pointed to the jukebox, then made a cutting motion across his throat.

Mike nodded and went to pull the plug on the jukebox.

"Say it again," the man on the stage said.

"Can I sing a song?"

"What song?"

"One I wrote last night."

He laughed. "That your parents over there?"

I glanced toward the bar, when Mom and Dad watched me.

"Yeah, I'm Charley Eye."

"No kidding?" He held out his hand to me.

When I took it, he yanked me onto the stage. "I'm Billy Dreadnaught. I heard you on the radio when you sang *Wendy*."

"Did you like it?"

"Hell, yeah. What'cha got for tonight?"

"*They Call the Wind Maria*."

"All right. You start, and we'll back you up."

"I need a guitar."

"Take mine. I got a spare in the back."

I raised the microphone two inches, then strummed a few notes.

Billy came back, adjusting the strap of his spare guitar over his shoulder.

I played and sang the song, then I did '*Your Cheatin' Heart*.'

The people at the bar and tables stopped talking to listen.

The drummer picked up the beat, then the bass guitarist joined in.

We got a nice round of applause when we finished.

*Thank you, Hank Williams.*

"You got anything else?" Billy asked.

"Yeah, a couple more."

I did *Heartaches by the Number*, then *The Battle of New Orleans*. That one got a few people on the dance floor.

I then started playing *Boot Scootin' Boogie*. After a few lines, I jumped to the dance floor and began doing a line dance as I continued to play the guitar. I motioned for the people to line up with me to dance across the floor and back again. Mom and Dad came to join the line. The steps were easy to learn, and soon everyone was moving together.

Little did they know, I'd performed this same set of numbers thirty times or more when I was in my forties.

*Or when I will be in my forties, I guess.*

* * * * *

The 45 rpm records would hit the market soon, and I hoped to be discovered by a record company before then.

RCA Victor would be selling their automatic record players for $12.50, and the records would cost 69 cents. That wasn't a lot, but if Dad could work out a deal where we'd earn a commission of a few cents on each record sold, we could be making thousands of dollars when the 45s came out.

That night, after we got back from the bar and

everyone was asleep, I slipped out to the barn to do some research on the 45 rpm records and portable record players to go with them.

The battery was fully charged; the solar panels worked well.

On Wikipedia, I found the RCA Victor Company would start producing the 45s in 1948, just two years away. I knew from my experience in the 1950s, jukeboxes would change over to the 45s, and thousands of the machines were in bars, cafes, and malt shops across the country. By the mid-50s, half the teenage girls in the U. S. would have one of RCA's record players in their bedrooms, along with a collection of 45 rpm records containing their favorite songs.

I had to be ready for the 45s.

By 1950, we could be making thousands of dollars a month. In addition to that, I would 'invent' a few things, like the remote TV controller, Super Glue, power steering, videotape recorders, Mr. Potato Head, hula hoops, transistor radios...

I'd then invest all the profits into solar cells, wind turbines, and electric-powered cars.


* * * * *


I bought a page of three-cent stamps, then sat at the kitchen table addressing envelopes.

The first one went to Frances Crick and James Watson at Cambridge University, England. Inside the envelope was my rendition of the double helix along with their detailed description of DNA that they would present to the world eight years in the future; 1953. This would give them a jump-start on winning the Nobel Prize in Medicine.

The next letter went to Dr. Jonas Salk at the University of Michigan in Ann Arbor. I sent him the complete chemical structure of his 'killed virus' vaccine he developed in 1955.

I also printed out the chemical formula for thalidomide, the drug widely prescribed as a tranquilizer for pregnant women in the 1950s. I also included detailed descriptions of birth defects caused by the drug. This I sent to the Chemie Gruenethal company, developer of the medicine, in Germany.

Next was a letter to President Harry S. Truman telling him that the North Koreans would invade South Korea in 1950. I didn't expect anyone to pay any attention to such a prediction, but I sent copies of the letter to Robert Porter Patterson, Secretary of War and the Secretary of State, James Francis Byrnes. Maybe someone in one of those departments would tie the information into other intelligence about North Korea.

I sent several more letters detailing scientific and medical breakthroughs coming in the 1950s.

Dad dropped the letters in a mailbox in Springfield. I didn't include my name or a return address because people might track me down and throw me in an insane asylum. I knew from reading history that these things happened to 'crazy people'.

The one letter where I did give my name and address was addressed to Lou Ottens in Bellingwolde, Holland. I included an external sketch of the cassette tape player he would invent in the 1960s. I didn't include the inner workings of the device, but offered the details to him if he would collaborate with me in producing my music on tape. I reasoned that the engineer was already thinking about his invention that would become hugely successful and propel Sony to worldwide fame and fortune.

* * * * *

At the next Saturday night show, I played two new songs; *Proud Mary* and *Love Grows (Where my Rosemary Goes)*.

Melody on the drums and Dolly with her sax made a big improvement in the performances.

Halfway through *Proud Mary*, the five cheerleaders ran to the floor and began their routine, which by now was smooth and coordinated.

Mary and Rose Mary were very pleased with their songs. Now all five girls had their own songs.

After I played *Sugar Sugar*, I motioned for them to come up on stage.

I knew they loved to do *Y M C A*, so I started with that, and they lined up behind me to perform.

They stayed on stage for the rest of the show, making it a great performance.

At the break, I told Dad we should pay the five girls.

"What?"

"They're doing a wonderful job."

"How much?" Dad asked.

"Maybe ten dollars apiece."

"Holy cow, son, that's fifty bucks."

"Okay, how about seven?"

"How much is that?"

"Thirty-five dollars"

"What do you think, Mom?" he asked.

"It's a fine idea. And if they're going to perform every Saturday night, I'll make them some matching

136

outfits."

"Good idea," I said. "They'll love that."

When I went on stage for the second half, I waved the girls up on the stage.

"All right, ladies. You're getting seven bucks each for tonight's work."

They were almost ecstatic at the prospect of earning money, and I got a fist bump from each one.

"Here we go with *Brandy*, then *Wendy*."

I followed that with *California Girls*.

* * * * *

The audience in the Casa Loma Ballroom in St. Louis was the largest I'd ever seen; a thousand people or more.

I adjusted the mic, then spoke into it. "Where's my posse?"

Wendy waved to me from the third row. Brandy, Mary, Rosemary, and Caroline sat with her.

"Get up here, ladies."

They stood and hurried to the steps at the end of the stage. In the frilly turquoise and pink costumes Mom had made for them, they looked very pretty and professional. And now they were making twelve dollars a night, plus travel expenses.

Melody and Dolly each made twenty a night.

I gave the posse the sequence of the first six numbers we'd perform. They nodded their understanding and formed a line ten feet behind me.

We started off with *California Girls*, then did *Wendy*.

The girls knew them quite well and had worked out their own dance steps. The audience loved it.

I follow *Wendy* with *Brandy, Proud Mary, Love Grows (Where My Rosemary Goes), Sweet Caroline,* and then *Johnny B Goode*.

As the audience applauded, I turned and whispered, "Y M C A."

"Yes!" Wendy said as they spread themselves apart.

About the middle of the piece, I saw a man come down the aisle, then walk over in front of Mom and Dad, where they sat in the front row.

He knelt down in front of Dad and whispered to him. Mom leaned in to hear what he was saying.
My brothers sat in the four seats to Mom's right. She said something to D.L., and he made his normal sour face, then went to sit on the floor in front of James. Mom moved over to the seat vacated by D.L. and motioned for the man to sit between her and Dad.

By the time we finished *Y M C A*, most of the people were on their feet, performing the moves with the cheerleaders behind me. My brothers got into it, too, even D.L.

When we finished the song, I announced a ten-minute break. We got a nice ovation as the girls gave me high-fives and left the stage.

I went to see what was up with the guy talking to Mom and Dad.

"This is Mr. Wainwright," Mom said.

"I'm glad to meet you, Charley Eye. You put on a great show."

"Thank you." I glanced at Dad.

"Mr. Wainwright is a talent scout for RCA Victor." Dad's smile was almost as big as Mr. Wainwright's.

"Really?" I held out my hand to him. "I've been waiting for you."

# Chapter Nine

I felt a *whoosh*, like a stream of time flowing through a twisting tube, making me dizzy and confused. I woke to the sound of Caitlion's soft words.

"...and I got crispy butterflies."

The light was dim, a muted bluish color. Soothing.

I smiled. *Crispy butterflies?*

When I leaned forward, the hospital bed raised behind me, supporting my back.

"You..." Dry throat. Scratchy. I swallowed.

"Try a sip of your Coke."

The straw in my drink was flat and wide, easy to draw the double stream of tangy liquid into my mouth.

"Ah, better," I said. "You changed clothes."

"Just the color."

She touched a blinking panel that curved around her left forearm. Her skintight outfit slowly changed from mint green to baby blue, starting at her neck and flowing down to her feet in a soft cascade of changing colors.

"Beautiful."

She touched another button on the panel. "A little cool. I'll click it up to 73 degrees."

Her hair was pastel lavender, long and braided, with strings of tiny, glittering droplets of light intertwined with the strands of hair. Precise bangs curved across her forehead just above her violet eyebrows.

"I thought your eyes were brown?"

Another touch on the control panel. "How about blue for a sunny day?"

I watched, amazed, as her eyes faded through shades of gray, then to sky blue, and finally Caribbean blue.

"Wow. Nice."

"You ready for your burger?" She opened a translucent container, where a Big Mac and crispy butterflies nestled in a bed of fluffy white lettuce.

I took the burger from her. "It's still hot."

"I set the box at 96 degrees."

"Perfect." I took a bite, savoring the tangy flavor.

"How are you feeling?" She glanced at a cushioned chair near the wall, then nodded toward the bed. It rolled forward, positioned itself beside my bed, then turned toward her. She sat and crossed her legs. It adjusted upward to bring her to my eye-level.

"Great," I said.

"They did the four-forty upgrade."

"Four-forty?"

"Heart, both lungs, liver, and the pancreas. While you were out, the doc asked if they should replace the prostate while they had you opened up. I told her it was probably worn out, so to go ahead. I hope that's all right."

"Um...sure."

"All the new organs are warranted for fifty years, the heart for seventy-five." She took a sip of my Coke. "And the caldeauem batteries have a lifetime charge."

This information was delivered so mater-of-factly as she touched a compartment on the inside of my burger box to uncover a pool of steaming ketchup, it seemed commonplace to her. But I was blown away.

*My major organs replaced? Good for fifty more years. What the hell? A few minutes ago, I was dying.*

I chewed a bite of butterfly-shaped fries with hot

ketchup. "How long since they finished the...um...four-forty?"

She took one of the butterfries. "It's been almost an hour. The surgeon wants you walking before rain. Then out the door by sunset."

"Rain?" I sipped my Coke and handed it back to her.

She looked at me as if I should know this. "Every Monday and Thursday at four? Thirty minutes of rain? Maybe I should defrag your memory tonight after you go to sleep."

"Maybe. What's in this Coke?"

"I had it fortified with your daily requirements of vitamins and minerals. Does it taste okay?"

"Yeah, great. Do I get a suit like yours?"

"It's on the way. I didn't order it until I was sure of your new waist size."

"Oh, good. I wouldn't want to look fat like you."

"Shut up."

"How much do I weigh?"

She glanced at a LED display on the bed. "One-sixty."

"Will my suit be air-conditioned?"

"That's standard. But we call them 'symskins.'"

"Right. Now I remember. How's the air outside?"

"The air?"

"Yeah. Smoggy?"

"Smoggy?"

"Dirty, grimy."

"The air's fine. Clean and clear."

"The icecaps?"

"What about them?"

"Are they melting?"

She reached to touch a control panel on my left

forearm, bringing it to life.

*Where did that come from?*

I glanced around, realizing I wasn't hooked up to any tubes or wires.

"Ninety-eight-point-six temp," she said. "Blood sugar a little high. I'll adjust that. Blood pressure good. Ah, here's the problem. You still have twenty-six percent of the anesthesia in your system. That'll soon filter out, and your brain will start to function at normal levels. The icecaps, as far as I know, are the same as they've been for past five centuries. Why do you ask?"

"Just curious." I smiled and bit into my Big Mac. *Ummm...delicious. Some things never change.*

"This is really good," I mumbled around a mouthful. "How long till rain?"

"Forty-five minutes. Don't forget, my flute recital is tonight."


The End

If you enjoyed reading Do Not Resuscitate please leave a brief review on Amazon

Thank you.

Like me on Facebook → Facebook/charleybrindley

charleybrindley@yahoo.com

www.charleybrindley.com

Charley Brindley is a retired coder living in the Ozarks of southwest Missouri. He draws on his experiences in the U. S. Air Force and extensive world travels to write adventure novels.

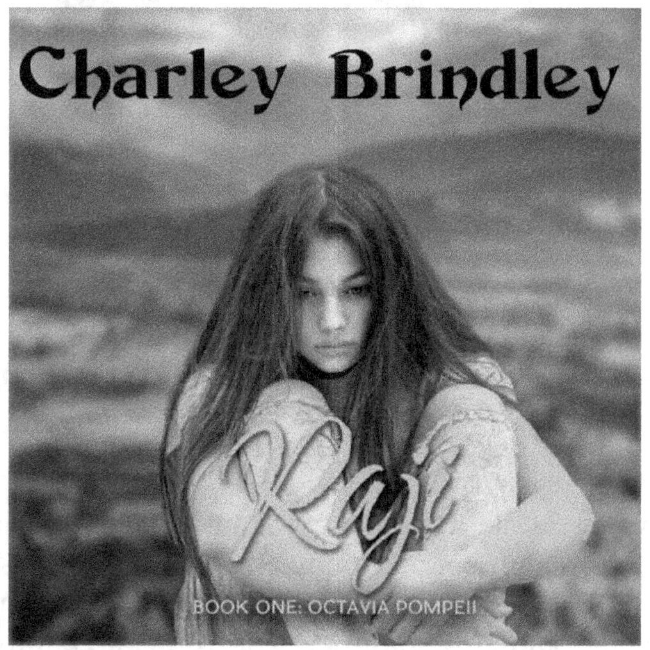


1.

*Raji Book One: Octavia Pompeii*

December 1925. Vincent Fusilier finds Raji sleeping in his parents' barn. He thinks she's a vagrant and tells her she has to go. She doesn't understand English and doesn't know where she is. Over the next few months, these two teens struggle to understand each other's language and culture.

2.

*Raji Book Two: The Academy*

August 1926. Raji is accepted into the prestigious Octavia Pompeii Academy. She and Elizabeth Keesler are the only girls in the student body of one hundred cadets and must endure the derision and taunts from ninety-eight boys who would like nothing better than to see them drop out of school. In addition to the contempt of the male students and high academic standards set by the instructors, Raji and Elizabeth must also conform to the strict disciplinary code enforced by the indomitable Elvira Gulch, Director of Development.

3.

*Raji Book Three: Dire Kawa*

*October 1932.* At the beginning of the Great Depression, schools and universities all over America were cutting back and even closing their campuses. Raji and Fuse, like so many other young people, were to be cut adrift. Having concentrated on nothing but academics for the past four years, they were not prepared for the brutal economic realities of a world sinking into misery and hopelessness.

4.

*Raji Book Four: The House of the West Wind*

Fuse returns to Burma in 1941 to look for Kayin. He left Raji behind in Virginia to recuperate from her ordeal, but she promised to join him later in Mandalay. It has been eight years since Fuse and Raji left Burma on the ill-fated training mission to Ethiopia. Since then, he has not heard anything from Kayin. She is probably married by now, or at least in a relationship with someone, but he has to find out, just to be sure she's all right. What he discovers at the old hotel is something completely unexpected.

148

5.

*Oxana's Pit*

Oxana uses forced labor to operate an illegal amber mine in the Amazon. Her open-pit excavation is on land owned by Tosh Scarborough. When he discovers Oxana's pit on a satellite photo, he goes to investigate and is captured by Oxana's thugs. One of Tosh's employees, Amber Bravant, organizes a search for him. Oxana is quick to punish and even murder her slave laborers, but what will happen if she gets her hands on Amber?

6.

*Ariion XXIII*

Ariion Sanders, a disabled teenage girl, is inspired by a homeless man she meets in a New York City jail. The man, Cameron Littleheart St. Lawrence, has been arrested for bank robbery, but without convincing evidence, the judge is forced to release him. The bumbling bank robbers have their loot stolen from them, and they think Cameron took it. After they kidnap Cameron, Ariion hatches a plan for his rescue; however, her scheme goes awry, and she finds herself in deep trouble.

7.

## Cian

Cian and Saxon's meeting in the heart of the Amazon is more than an encounter of two people; it's the coming together of two different worlds. Their explorations and adventures take them deep into the rain forest, then halfway around the globe in search of a peaceful place to settle down. But instead of finding peace, their shared sense of justice finds them traveling from Europe to New York, then back to Brazil, where they must confront the evil network of the ambitious and heartless Oxana, who will stop at nothing to advance her trade in endangered animals, as well as women and little girls.

8.

*The Last Seat on the Hindenburg*

A misdialed phone number brings Donovan to Sandia's front door. He thought he was to teach Braille to a blind person, while she thought he was a disability attorney. When Donovan learns of Sandia's and her grandfather's dreadful circumstances, the Braille lesson is forgotten and he embarks on a mission to help Sandia solve the several dilemmas that threaten to overwhelm her.

9.

*The Sea of Tranquility 2.0: Book One*

An exasperated high school social science teacher with half her senior class failing, resorts to a drastic measure, resulting in The Sea of Tranquility 2.0. Four of her students come up with a radical project to help slow rising sea levels and provide a homeland for some of the millions of refugees set adrift by wars, failing economies, and gang violence.

10.

*The Sea of Tranquility 2.0: Book Two*

Monica, Harry, and Caitlion try to find a way to communicate with the Jamori nomads they left behind in the Safandel Desert. While working hard to finish their senior year of high school, they're also working on details of their plan to gain funding for the Sea of Tranquility 2.0 project.

11.

*The Sea of Tranquility 2.0 Book Three: The Sand Vipers*

When Sikandar's homeland is invaded, he must return to defend his people. Monica defies him, refusing to stay behind, insisting she will not lose him again. The two of them, plus the Gang of Four, set off for the remote and desolate outback of Alcina Sahar, where Sikandar is certain his people have taken refuge.

12.

*The Sea of Tranquility 2.0 Book Four: The Republic*
Monica and Sikandar, along with the Gang of Eight, open the first pipeline to siphon seawater to the Sea of Tranquility 2.0. Will it work? Scientists are divided on the theory of a nine-foot wide pipe reaching 156 miles across the desert that will actually pull water from the ocean unassisted by any pumps. If it works, the new City of Tranquility will flourish; if not, the desert will reclaim what little work has been done.

13.

*Dragonfly vs Monarch: Book One*

Autumn Willow is a grad student at MIT. In her spare time, she co-pilots her grandfather's B-17, a restored WWII bomber. Sasha Brezhnev is a pilot for the Russian Air Force, flying the SU-57 fighter jet. She is assigned seek-and-destroy missions over the Safandel Desert in central Anddor Shallau, where terrorists are covertly working to destroy the country's democratic government. Rigger Entime is an engineer working on a CIA project to develop a tiny drone aircraft to be used in surveillance and possibly carry out assassinations of terrorists' leaders.

14.

***Dragonfly vs Monarch: Book Two***

The Dragonfly and Monarch are tiny drone aircrafts designed to resemble actual insects. They can flitter around military installations and terrorists' camps without being noticed while they collect video data about these installations and the people in charge. On their first mission over an isolated stretch of desert, their remote pilots, one American and one Russian, are drawn into a strange struggle to survive. In their attempt to retrieve their disabled drones, the pilots discover a shocking secret about themselves.

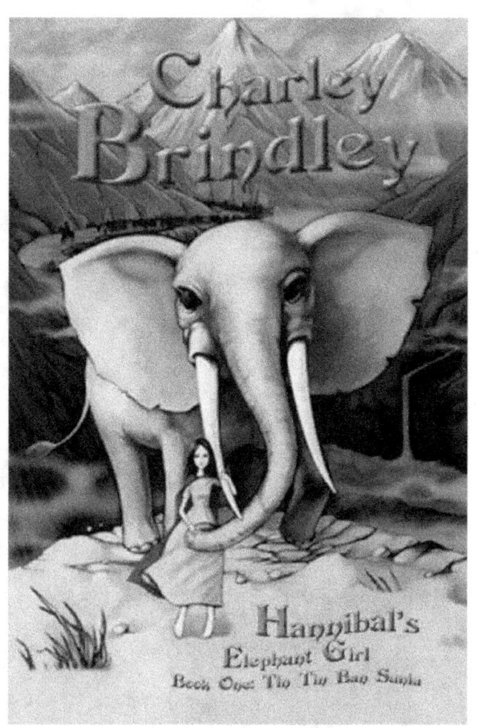

15.

*Hannibal's Elephant Girl*

In 218 BCE, Hannibal took his army, along with 27 elephants, over the Alps to attack the Romans. Eleven years before this historic event, on the banks of a river near Carthage, in North Africa, one of his elephants pulled a drowning girl from the turbulent waters. Thus began Liada's epic journey with the elephant known as Obolus.

16.

Hannibal's Elephant Girl, Book Two
The Voyage to Iberia

Liada and the slave girl, Tin Tin Ban Sunia, sail away from Carthage with Hannibal, on their way to Iberia. Also on board is Obolus, Hannibal's prized war elephant. Not only do they have to deal with pirates and Roman galleys, Sulobo the slave master and Sukal the javelineer are on the ship, too, just waiting for a chance to wreak vengeance on the two girls.

*Sea of Sorrows*

An old man returns to Thailand after a fifty-year absence. When he was in Bangkok on leave from the Vietnam War, he met a girl and fell in love. After returning to the battlefield, he was critically wounded and shipped to a hospital in San Diego. After recovering from his injuries he goes back to Bangkok looking for Chayan, but she's not there. A year later he returns and one of the other girls tells him Chayan died during a typhoid epidemic. Devastated, he returns to the States, goes to medical school and eventually starts a family. Now, after fifty years, he goes again to Bangkok, but instead of Chayan, he finds his past had been evolving without him.

18.

### *The Last Mission of the Seventh Cavalry*

A unit of the Seventh Cavalry is on a mission over Afghanistan when their plane is hit by something. The soldiers bail out of the crippled plane, but when the thirteen men and women reach the ground, they are not in Afghanistan. Not only are they four thousand miles from their original destination but it appears they have descended two thousand years into the past where primitive forces fight each other with swords and arrows. The platoon is thrown into a battle where they must choose sides quickly or die. They are swept along in a tide of events so powerful that their courage, ingenuity and weapons are tested to the limits of their durability and strength.

19.

## *Do Not Resuscitate*

A dying man tells his great granddaughter that he has signed a Do Not Resuscitate document, giving instructions for medical personal to let him die if he's determined to be brain dead. He's invited on a long journey that he thinks is taking place in his subconscious mind as his body is being kept alive against his wishes. What unfolds before him may be an elaborate hallucination caused by the psychedelic effect of the anticholinergic drugs being pumped through his body, or are these strange and cathartic events actually happening?

20.

*Henry IX*

The queen of England is 93 years old. The process of installing a new monarch is already being organized.

Her son, Prince Charles, is the heir apparent. However, someone is attempting to alter the line of succession.

There are over 140 people in line to become monarch. If Prince Charles is for any reason, unable to ascend, then the next in line, Prince William, will become King. If he is unavailable, Prince George will be next in line, and so on, down the list.

Evil plans are being executed.

Lady Poinciana Victoria Lancaster, known to her friends as 'Ciana', is number thirty-seven. William George Tindall Mountbatten is number thirty-eight on the list of Royals.

Wearing a disguise and going by the name of 'Scipio' William Mountbatten accidentally meets Ciana in a London pub.

Long ago, a general famously said, 'All battle plans fall apart upon first contact with the enemy.' That is exactly what happened when Ciana and Scipio come together.

21. 

Qubit's Incubator

Catalina Saylor is allowed to work in Qubit's Incubator on probation for thirty days. If she proves her idea within that time, she will be allowed to stay and try to obtain a patent on her device.

Qubit's Incubator is a work place for bright people with good ideas who have no resources to develop their ideas.

If they are accepted, they will be provided with a workspace, equipment, and other benefits for thirty days. If they are not successful within that time, they will leave with nothing.

22.

*The Rod of God, Book One: The Edge of Disaster*

Staff Sergeant Saxon "Pagan" McKenzie and Tech Sergeant William "Choir Boy" Kabilis are involved in a nuclear accident during the Cuban Missile Crisis. Not only does it threaten to set off World War III, but it sends McKenzie and Kabilis on a journey into the first days of the  Vietnam War.


Coming Soon


23. *Dragonfly vs Monarch, Book Three*

Theodore Breckinridge (Pug) and Rio Lujan join forces to rescue Autumn and **Sasha**.


24. *Hannibal's Elephant Girl: Book Three*

Liada and her friend, Tin Tin Ban Sunia, struggle to fit into their new environment in Iberia.


25. *Still Waters Run Deep*

A precious five-year-old girl is accidentally imbedded with five gigabytes of medical information.

26. *Ms Machiavelli*

The teenage daughter of the famous Italian, Nioccolo

Machiavelli, makes her mark during the Renaissance.

27. *The Last Mission of the Seventh Cavalry, Book Two*

The soldiers of the Seventh must mount a rescue mission for the stranded astronauts after they came down from the International Space Station in the escape pod.

28. *Ariion XXIX*

In the year 2219 Ariion XXIX is her third rotation as quadrant perimeter analog. She has jurisdiction along the outer beacons of our solar sphere, encompassing all ten planets and their moons, both natural and artificial. She is the 29th Ariion in a long line Ariions stretching back to the first Ariion, born in Valdacia in the year 221 BCE.

29. *The Journey to Valdacia*

A satellite cartographer has discovered on his latest photos, the ruins of an ancient city in the Sahara Desert. It has been uncovered by a recent sandstorm and Donny slips away from his job at xxx to go explore the ruins before anyone else, especially his colleague, Kelli, spots the location of what appears to be a very large city. Before he can reach the ruins, he's entangled in secret and deadly activity.

* 9 7 8 8 8 3 5 4 1 1 0 4 8 *